Maddie hac

death as the giant stranger called Blade.

The west door was not yet fully open when he grabbed his pistol-grip shotgun and pivoted, his right hand on the grip, his finger on the trigger, and his left hand on the pump. He worked the slide action so fast his arm blurred, the three booming shots thundering as one.

Rafe took the first shot in the face, a full load of buckshot that exploded his head in a gory shower of flesh, blood and brains. He literally died before he knew what hit him.

The second blast caught Bo in the throat and nearly decapitated him, his ruptured neck spattering his companions and the floor, his face cemented in a mask of shock as he crumpled.

Only Clem managed to snap off a shot from his revolver, and in his haste he missed. Blade did not. The buckshot tore into Clem's chest, the impact lifting him off his feet and hurling him out the doorway to sprawl on his back on the dirt outside. He wheezed and gurgled and tried to rise onto his elbows, blood spurting from his ravaged torso and mouth, then collapsed and died.

"Son of a bitch!" someone exclaimed.

Also in the Blade series:

#1: FIRST STRIKE
#2: OUTLANDS STRIKE
#3: VAMPIRE STRIKE
#4: PIPELINE STRIKE
#5: PIRATE STRIKE

DAVID ROBBINS

LEISURE BOOKS NEW YORK CITY

Dedicated to —
Judy and Joshua and Shane.
To Wally,
the best friend a man ever had.
And to Debie,
for the bulldozer.

A LEISURE BOOK®

February 1990

Published by

Dorchester Publishing Co., Inc.
276 Fifth Avenue
New York, NY 10001

Printed in the United States of America.

CHAPTER ONE

Maddie intuitively sensed trouble brewing, serious trouble, the kind that frequently resulted in violence and death. After three years on the job she could read the atmosphere in the Booze N' Broads like an expert tracker could read animal prints in the mud or snow. She knew there would be trouble, and she knew who would be the cause.

"Fill 'er up again, sweetheart!" came the lusty cry from one of the three grungy men clustered at the east end of the bar.

Reluctantly Maddie complied, walking over and reaching for his mug.

With a flick of his left arm, quick as a striking rattler, the customer grabbed her right wrist. "Hold on there, honey," he said, leering and winking. "Are you lookin' for a good time?"

Maddie looked into his bloodshot eyes. "What if I am?"

He puffed up his chest and chuckled. "Then you want a real man to show you how to have some fun!"

Slowly, aware the other patrons were watching the exchange, Maddie used her green eyes to rake the lean braggart from his thatch of brown hair, over his deer-hide shirt and wool pants, to his scuffed brown boots. "I sure do," she agreed, grinning, hoping her humor would defuse his arrogance. "Know where I can find one?"

A peal of laughter erupted from the dozen onlookers. Everyone laughed except the man seated at a table situated in the southeast corner of the room, his huge form shrouded in shadows.

Maddie flinched as the pressure on her wrist increased, and she saw the customer's brown eyes narrow angrily. "Do you want a refill or not?" she demanded.

"Maybe I want more than another brew," he said.

She refused to be intimidated by his belligerence. Experience had taught her that if she gave a drunk an inch, he'd take a mile. "There are three pros in the back. Pay the fee and you can have all the fun you can handle."

"Maybe I don't want a damned whore."

"Whatever. Just let go of my wrist."

The braggart jerked his face closer to hers, causing her ribs to gouge the edge of the bar. "Maybe I want you," he declared.

His buddies snickered.

Maddie gritted her teeth and tried to pull her wrist free, but the braggart was too strong for her. Fortunately the bar separated them, or he would be pawing her body. She'd seen his type countless times, and regrettably they were drawn to her in the same slavering manner as a starving bear to sweet honey. Her shoulder-length blonde hair, her lively blue eyes, her clean complexion and voluptuous figure all conspired to make her a prime target for every lecher in the Outlands. "Mister, I don't think you've ever been in here before, so I'll give you fair warning. The owner doesn't allow the customers to lay a hand on the bartenders."

"He doesn't, huh?"

"No."

"Is this owner here?"

"No," Maddie admitted, "but the bouncer is."

He made a show of surveying the dimly lit room. Canvas covered the sole window, and six lanterns provided feeble light. "What bouncer?"

Where the hell was the Kid? Maddie wondered, gazing at the empty stool near the middle of the west wall. Brount would have a fit if the braggart caused any damage to the establishment or harmed any of Brount's employees. She mustered a halfhearted smile and attempted to placate the swine holding her. "Look, we don't want any trouble. Why don't you relax, and I'll give you a brew on the house."

The braggart glanced at his burly companions. All three bore the unmistakable stamp of hard-bitten men accustomed to having their own way. Their ragged clothes were caked with dust. Each one wore a gun belt, and the burly pair were also armed with rifles, one with a Marlin slung over his left shoulder, the other with a Winchester in his brawny hands.

"The bitch doesn't want any trouble," the braggart said sarcastically.

"I don't like her attitude, Clem," stated the man holding the Winchester.

"Me neither," agreed the third man.

Clem snickered and placed his right hand on Maddie's chin. "I guess it's unanimous. If you don't want to be polite, we'll have to teach you some manners."

"I'm warning you—" Maddie began, but his right hand clamped on her throat, choking off her air, and she gasped as he slipped his left hand under her right arm and heaved, hauling her onto the top of the bar, her legs knocking several glasses and mugs to the wooden floor with a noisy crash.

"*You're* warnin' *me*?" Clem demanded, his features livid, his nose an inch from hers.

Maddie struggled, striving to pry his fingers from her throat to no avail.

"Nobody tells me what to do!" Clem snapped. "Nobody!"

"Let's poke her," suggested the one who had the Marlin over his shoulder.

"I bet she'd be real tasty," added the third.

"I'd better let her live then," Clem said, and released his hold on her throat, pleased when she gasped and clutched at her neck, savoring her torment. He liked to see his women squirm and whimper before he poked them.

Maddie sat up, inhaling deeply, calculating whether she could reach the revolver kept under the bar, lying on a shelf 20 feet from her position. If she tried, she knew Clem would shoot her. She also knew better than to expect any help from the other customers. Minding one's own business was an unspoken law of the Outlands, and anyone foolish enough to violate the rule ran the risk of being planted in a shallow grave.

Clem stared at her green sweater and faded jeans. "Nice threads you've got there, gorgeous. There isn't a hole in them." He paused, studying her chest, and licked his thin lips. "What's under there?"

Her blood went cold, and she started to scramble away from him, but he grabbed her sweater and yanked, tumbling her onto the floor at his feet. She landed on her hands and knees, and before she could rise his left hand descended on her hair.

"Stand, bitch!" Clem spat, and brutally wrenched on her golden tresses, pulling her erect.

An inadvertent cry escaped her lips. She grimaced and swatted at his left arm.

"Be nice," Clem said mockingly.

A grizzled patron rose and headed for the front door.

"Where the hell do you think you're going, Gramps?" demanded Clem's friend with the Winchester.

The patron halted and faced the trio, visibly blanching. "Out for a little fresh air, is all."

"Your fresh air can wait. Sit down until we tell you different," declared Clem's buddy.

"Sure thing," the patron said, and took a seat at the nearest table.

"That's tellin' him, Bo," Clem commented.

Bo laughed and hefted the Winchester. "Anyone else who would like to leave?" he asked, and when no one responded he threw back his head and cackled. "We've got us a bunch of wimps here, Clem. This will be easy pickings."

"Please!" Maddie said. "Get out of here before it's too late!"

"Too late for what?" Clem replied, and snorted. "Honey, we're just gettin' fired up."

"Is there any kind of law in this town, darling?" Bo inquired.

Maddie refused to reply.

"They ain't got no law hereabouts," stated the man with the Marlin. "I'd stake my life on it."

"Then let's get down to business," Clem said, and planted his mouth on Maddie's forehead, kissing her, flicking his wet tongue across her skin, then smacking his lips when he straightened. "Ummmm. Yummy. She *is* tasty."

Maddie clenched her fists at her sides and trembled, more from simmering rage than fear. Revulsion swamped her as she felt his saliva trickling down her forehead onto her nose. "You're disgusting!" she blurted.

"You'll change your tune by the time I'm done," Clem assured her, smirking.

"You take her first," Bo prompted. "I'll go second, and Rafe third."

"Why do I always got to go last?" Rafe asked.

"Because you're the ugliest," Bo said, and chortled.

"There's enough of her to go around," Clem said, and reached for her right breast.

"*That's enough*!"

The two words, spoken with the explosive force of a cannon, froze the patrons in their chairs and caused Clem, Bo, and Rafe to spin toward the source, Bo with his rifle leveled. All three focused on the table in the shadows at the southeast corner.

"Who the hell?" Clem snapped.

The speaker addressed them again in a lower, menacing,

tone. "Leave the woman alone."

"Are you talkin' to us?" Clem asked in disbelief, shocked to find anyone possessing the gall to oppose them.

"You're the bastards picking on an unarmed woman."

Clem's right hand twitched, and he almost drew the Smith and Wesson 459 strapped to his right hip. Two factors dissuaded him. First, he couldn't determine whether the man in the corner already had a weapon trained on them. Second, the man's voice contained an authoritative quality, a certain distinctive iron edge that hinted at swift retribution if his words were ignored. "Why don't you step out where we can see you, mister?" Clem challenged him.

The stranger gave no reply.

"What's the matter?" Bo taunted. "Are you scared, big mouth?"

A protracted sigh issued from the corner, and then the speaker rose, and seemed to go on rising and rising until he reached his full stature of seven feet. Casually, calmly, he moved into the light, exposing his huge form to their view.

"Son of a bitch!" Bo exclaimed.

Clem blinked a few times, stunned at the sight of a veritable giant attired in a black leather vest, green fatigue pants, and black combat boots. The giant's physique was awesome; his chest and arms bulged with muscles, layer upon layer of rippling, latent power. About his narrow waist were strapped a pair of Bowie knifes. Crisscrossing his broad chest were two bandoliers, the loops crammed with shotgun shells. And in his right hand, held with the ease with which a child might hold a small toy, was a Mossberg pistol-grip shotgun. He advanced to within ten feet and halted.

"You shouldn't go stickin' your nose in where it doesn't belong," Bo told the giant.

"Yeah," Rafe added. "We don't cotton to busybodies."

The giant, oddly enough, grinned. "Are you trying to scare me?"

"Don't make fun of us!" Clem stated angrily. "No one

messes with us. Anyone with half a brain knows we're as mean as a flock of rattlesnakes!"

"A flock!" the giant repeated quizzically, then nodded. "Oh. You must mean the winged variety."

Bo glanced at Clem. "He's makin' fun of us again."

"I know," Clem declared harshly, debating his course of action. Although he wanted to tear into the giant and beat the man's smirking face to a pulp, he perceived the three of them would be no match for the interloper's obviously prodigious strength, and he disliked the idea of going up against a shotgun at close range. Taking the giant on in a frontal assault would be suicide, but who said they had to use a frontal assault? A sly grin creased his mouth, and he looked at the side door in the west wall, then at the front door located in the south wall approximately 30 feet to the giant's rear.

"Do we waste this bastard?" Rafe asked eagerly.

"Nope," Clem said.

"What?" Rafe responded in surprise.

"We're leavin'," Clem announced, and proceeded to stalk from the premises, wisely skirting the giant by two yards.

Bo and Rafe, clearly flustered, hastened after their partner.

"What the hell are you doing?" Bo demanded. "We ain't never run from anybody before."

"Shut your face," Clem hissed.

The trio departed through the front door, Clem slamming the door after them.

Maddie stared at the giant, who had warily watched the three troublemakers depart, admiring his rugged, handsome features. He turned toward her, and she noted the comma of dark hair hanging above his right brow and the intensity of his gray eyes. "Thank you," she said.

"Are you all right?"

"Nothing hurt but my dignity," Maddie replied, and grinned self-consciously.

The patrons resumed their drinking and conversing, and

the subdued hum of conversation filled the room.

"Do you have to deal with scum like that often?" the giant asked.

"Scum? They just had a little too much to drink," Maddie said. "I see their kind in here all the time."

Her protector surveyed his surroundings and frowned distastefully. "This is no place for a lady."

"I work here," Maddie informed him a bit defensively.

He locked his unwavering gaze on her. "Still no place for a lady."

Feeling strangely uncomfortable, Maddie averted her face. "Yeah, well, a girl has to make a living, and being a bartender beats what those three women in the back are doing," she said, and jerked her left thumb at the corridor on the west side of the room. The bar ran along the entire width of the north wall, stopping six feet shy of the west wall, where the passage began that led back to the half-dozen narrow cubicles used by the prostitutes to ply their trade.

"What are they doing?" the giant asked.

She glanced at him to see if he was making fun of her, but to her astonishment she saw he was in earnest. "You don't know?"

"No."

"Didn't you hear me talking about the pros?"

"I didn't hear every word you spoke to that riffraff. I wasn't paying much attention until I saw him pull you onto the bar," the giant disclosed. "I do recall hearing the word pro before, but I—"

"It's short for prostitute. You know. A whore."

His expression rippled and solidified in stark disgust. "You mean there are women selling their bodies in the back?"

"That's what I mean, mister."

Sadness etched his eyes, and he uttered another of those pronounced sighs.

"Don't they have whores where you come from?" Maddie queried in jest, and received a major jolt when he answered.

"No."

"You're putting me on."

"No."

Intrigued by his unusual demeanor, her curiosity aroused to a fever pitch, Maddie gestured at the bar. "Look, you bailed me out of a tight fix. How about if I treat you to a drink?"

"I'm not thirsty," the giant said, and turned to leave. "Thanks anyway. Take care."

Maddie did a double take. She was accustomed to encountering men who regarded her more as a sex object than a person, men who ogled her overtly or covertly, men who tried to grope her, men who tried to impress her with their masculinity or a façade of gentlemanly behavior. Here was a man new to her experience, a man who came to her rescue but rebuffed her overture of gratitude. She wanted to get to know him, and she stepped closer and took hold of his arm. "Now hold on, mister. What harm can a drink do?"

He scrutinized her face for several seconds, then nodded. "Okay. You can treat me to a drink."

She grinned and walked around the west end of the bar. "What would you like?"

The giant strolled up to the bar and placed the shotgun on the counter, his gray eyes ranging over the assortment of bottles, jugs, and decanters lining the shelves on the north wall. "Do you have any milk?"

Impulsively, thinking he'd joked, Maddie laughed. "Milk? No, the cow died a week ago."

He frowned. "How about some fruit juice?"

Suddenly comprehending her protector's request was legitimate, Maddie adopted a serious expression and shook her head. "Sorry. We don't carry fruit juice. Booze and broads are the specialties here." She paused. "I doubt you could find any fruit in all of Shantytown."

He stared at her again with that look, that frank, questioning aspect, as if he attempted to gaze into the very depths of her soul. "Why do you live in Shantytown?"

"I was born here."

"Do you like it?"

The corners of Maddie's mouth curved downward. "Who in their right mind would like living in a pigsty?"

"Then why do you stay?"

She glimpsed a cockroach scuttling across the filthy floor and shrugged. "It's a matter of survival. Where else would I go?"

He leaned on the counter, the simple motion making his biceps and triceps swell, and spoke softly. "There's a whole world out there."

"Yeah, right. A world filled with mutations, radioactive toxins, and chemical poisons. A world where a woman on her own wouldn't last two minutes. Scavengers, raiders, and *worse* are everywhere. The Russians are reported to be south of us a ways. Where would I go if I left Shantytown, mister?"

The giant pursed his lips but didn't respond.

"I was born here, I'll die here," Maddie said morosely. "At least I had the common sense not to bring a child into this miserable world of ours."

"You don't want children?"

"Of course I do," Maddie declared bitterly, his queries agitating her, stirring emotions she'd erroneously believed had been long since eradicated. "But I'm not about to bring kids into this life to suffer and struggle in vain. All this world offers us is pain and more pain. I don't want to put a child through such a living hell."

"You've lived your entire life in the Outlands," he said, and somehow he conveyed a profound empathy for all the misery and heartache she had known.

She gaped at him for several seconds, then composed herself. "Where are my manners? I'm Maddie. Maddie Stender," she said, and offered her right hand.

"Blade," the giant responded, and took her slim hand in his enormous palm.

Maddie smiled, feeling the warmth of his skin against hers, surprised at the gentleness of his touch, knowing he could crush her hand with a slight constriction of his brawny fingers. "I'm pleased to meet you, Blade. You have an unusual name. I don't think I've ever met anyone called Blade before."

He released her hand. "I selected Blade as my name on my sixteenth birthday."

Maddie snickered. "Let me get this straight. You picked your own name?"

"At my Naming ceremony."

"I've never heard of such a thing," Maddie stated, and leaned toward him. "Where *are* you from?"

"Elsewhere."

"Far be it for me to pry," Maddie said, then motioned at the shelves. "Would you care for a beer instead of fruit juice."

"No, thanks," Blade answered. "I don't drink alcoholic beverages."

"You don't drink. . . ." Maddie began in disbelief, and shook her head. "Blade, I don't mind telling you I've never met a man like you."

"I'm not exceptional."

"I beg to differ," Maddie said, "and I should know because I've seen thousands of men pass through Shantytown. You're unique."

Her complaint elicited no reaction.

"Are you just passing through?" she asked him.

"I'm looking for someone," Blade divulged. "Perhaps you can help me find him."

"I'll do what I can. Does this person have a name?"

"I'm looking for a man named Dan Brount."

Maddie's mouth dropped, her astonishment self-evident. "Brount owns this tavern!"

"So I was told."

"Why are you looking for him?"

Blade's facial lines hardened and his eyes became steely. "My business with Brount is personal."

A chilling insight caused a tingle to run up and down her

spine, and Maddie involuntarily shivered. She abruptly comprehended that she stood in the presence of one of the most dangerous men she had ever met, perhaps *the* most dangerous, and she deduced his personal business with Daniel Brount did not bode well for Brount's life expectancy. Although Brount had hired her, she felt scant loyalty to the bastard.

"I was provided with a description of Brount," Blade went on, "and I intended to wait for him to arrive. Would he happen to be in the back?"

"No," Maddie said. "Brount is on a still run."

"A still run?"

"Yeah. He buys a lot of shine and home brew from the farmers and others, and he has to make a monthly inspection trip to make sure they'll meet their assigned quotas. He left early this morning."

Blade opened his mouth to speak.

With a resounding crash, startling every customer in the Booze N' Broads, the side door in the west wall flew inwards, the bright afternoon sun illuminating the floor space near the doorway, and into the tavern, into the space, charged Clem, Bo, and Rafe, all three with weapons leveled.

CHAPTER TWO

Gunfights were a common occurrence in Shantytown, brawls even more so, and fistfights almost a daily happening. Maddie Stender had witnessed dozen of each. She'd seen men react instinctively to a threatening foe, seen gun hands streak to holsters in the twinkling of an eye, had even seen the Kid in action four times, but never had she beheld anyone as adept at dispensing death as the giant stranger called Blade.

The west door was not yet fully open when he grabbed his pistol-grip shotgun and pivoted, his right hand on the grip, his finger on the trigger, and his left hand on the pump. He worked the slide action so fast his arm blurred, the three booming shots thundering as one.

Rafe took the first shot in the face, a full load of buckshot that exploded his head in a gory shower of flesh, blood, and brains. He literally died before he knew what hit him.

The second blast caught Bo in the throat and nearly decapitated him, his ruptured neck spattering his companions and the floor, his visage cemented in a mask of shock as he crumpled.

Only Clem managed to snap off a shot from his revolver,

and in his haste he missed. His adversary did not. The buckshot tore into Clem's chest, the impact lifting him from his feet and hurling him out the doorway to sprawl on his back on the dirt outside. He wheezed and gurgled and tried to rise onto his elbows, blood spurting from his ravaged torso and his mouth, then collapsed and died.

"Son of a bitch!" a customer exclaimed.

Blade straightened slowly and edged toward the three bodies, poking each with the tip of his right boot, insuring they were dead. He nudged Clem and turned.

Footsteps pounded in the hall leading to the cubicles, and a moment later a youth of 16 or 17 appeared and promptly halted at the end of the bar, his blue eyes widening at the sight of the carnage, while he strapped a gunbelt containing a matched pair of Ruger Redhawks around his thin waist. He wore a black shirt, black pants, and black boots. His brown hair hung to his narrow shoulders. "What the hell!" he cried, and found himself looking down the barrel of the Mossberg shotgun.

"Are you with them?" Blade demanded.

"Me? Hell, no! I don't know them," the youth responded.

Maddie came to the end of the bar. "Blade, this is Kid Zanto. He works here."

"Damn straight I do," the Kid snapped, and finished buckling his belt. "I'm the bouncer. It's my job to head off trouble like this."

"So where were you?" Blade asked.

Crimson flushed the Kid's face. "In the back," he mumbled, then suddenly became aggressive. "I'm supposed to be askin' the questions, mister. Blade, is it? What happened?"

Blade nodded at the corpses. "They suffered from a nutritional deficiency."

"What?"

"They needed more lead in their diet."

His forehead creased in perplexity, Kid Zanto glanced from the giant to the bodies and back. Understanding lit his eyes and he slapped his right thigh and laughed uproariously. ''Needed more lead! I get it! You're pretty clever.''

''Brount won't like this,'' Maddie mentioned.

The Kid's humor evaporated in an instant and he looked at her apprehensively. ''You won't rat on me, will you?''

''I won't tell Brount what you were doing when you should have been on duty,'' Maddie said, ''but he'll still be mad. You know how he is. Killings are bad for business.''

Kid Zanto chewed on his lower lip, then snapped his fingers. ''Maybe if I dump these stiffs, Brount will never find out.''

''Be serious,'' Maddie stated.

''Damn,'' the Kid said angrily, and cast a critical gaze on the stranger in the black leather vest. ''Who are you? Why'd you waste these jokers?''

''My name is Blade.''

''I know that!'' the Kid snapped. ''That's not what I meant and you know it! What are you doing here?''

''Vacationing,'' Blade said, and sauntered to the bar.

Kid Zanto clenched his fists, simmering with indignation, astounded anyone would treat him with such a cavalier attitude. During his two years as the bouncer at the Booze N' Broads he had handled over a hundred rough customers and slain nine men in gunfights. In Shantytown and for miles around his name inspired dread in those who might be inclined to challenge Brount's control, and he disliked being treated as a man of little consequence. He knew the customers were watching him and reasoned his reputation was on the line. ''Don't walk away from me when I'm talkin' to you,'' he warned the giant.

Blade, holding the Mossberg at his side, turned toward the gunman. ''Would you care for a drink? I'll treat.''

The unexpected offer partially mollified the Kid's anger. ''Sure. Why not? Provided you'll answer my questions.''

''If I can. I certainly wouldn't want to antagonize *you*,'' Blade said loudly, much louder than he had to, emphasizing the last word.

Kid Zanto's eyes narrowed. He knew everyone in the tavern had heard the giant, and he suspected the stranger had intended for everyone to hear, which meant Blade had deliberately given the patrons the impression that he respected the Kid's prowess. Why would the man do such a thing? the Kid asked himself, and hooked his thumbs in his gunbelt. "I'll have a whiskey," he announced, moving to the bar.

"Fine by me," Maddie said, "but aren't you forgetting something?"

"What?" the Kid responded.

Maddie pointed at the corpses.

"Damn. I forgot," Kid Zanto stated, and turned to scan the room. He spied a middle-aged pair of men off to the right huddled over a pitcher of beer. "Hey, Ed, Barney. How about doing me a favor?"

"What's that, Kid?" Ed Flanders, the tavern drunk, asked, his besotted mind not functioning with the greatest alacrity.

"How about if Barney and you haul these stiffs out to the dump?" the Kid proposed.

Barney Morris, a short man in torn jeans and a flannel shirt who worked at the Shantytown mill, frowned at the request. "No offense, Kid, but it's chilly out and the lousy dump is five miles from town. I'd rather pass."

"What if I let you pawn their belongings?"

Ed and Barney whispered for a full 15 seconds before replying.

"All right," Barney said.

"You got yourself a deal," Ed added.

Pleased at avoiding the distasteful task, the Kid grinned and glanced at Maddie. "How about that whiskey, gorgeous?"

"Brount won't like this," she reiterated, taking a glass and pouring into it the murky contents of a high-necked bottle.

"You let me worry about Danny," the Kid said.

Maddie deposited the glass on the counter. "I just hope he isn't in the same mood he was in when he left this morning. Something is bothering him. I can tell."

Kid Zanto took a sip of whiskey and felt the alcohol burn a path down his throat. "Yeah. I've noticed too." He faced the giant. "Now I want to know what you're doing here."

"He's only passing through town," Maddie responded quickly before Blade could answer.

"A drifter, huh?" Kid Zanto probed.

"That's right," Maddie said. "Another drifter."

The Kid glanced at her. "What are you? His mother? Let the man answer for himself," he stated, and returned his attention to Blade. "So what *are* you doing in Shantytown?"

"Passing through." Blade began reloading the Mossberg.

"Do you work for anybody?"

"I'm a drifter."

"Uh-huh," the Kid said, and swallowed more whiskey.

Barney Morris and Ed Flaunders were busily dragging the corpses outside. Ed frowned when he took hold of Rafe's arm and a squishy gob of brain matter smeared on his right hand.

"Tell me about Shantytown," Blade addressed Maddie.

"What do you want to know?"

"Everything."

Maddie leaned on her elbows, recalling the stories her loving grandmother had related when Maddie was very young. "I don't know everything, but I do know a little of Shantytown's history, which is probably no different from most of the towns in the Outlands. Let's see. World War Three occurred one hundred and six years ago, right?"

"Correct," Blade confirmed.

"Well, about the time of the war or shortly after, the government evacuated a lot of the folks from this area. The U.S. government, I think it was called."

"This area was once known as northern Wisconsin," Blade said, "and Wisconsin was one of fifty states in the United States of America, one of the leading superpowers in the world."

"Really?" Kid Zanto interjected. "I didn't know that.

What's a superpower?"

Blade looked at him. "A superpower was a nation that controlled or influenced many other nations."

"What was a nation?" the Kid asked.

"You haven't read many books on politics or history, have you?" Blade noted.

Kid Zanto and Maddie exchanged amazed expressions.

"You can read?" the Kid blurted.

"Yes."

"Books and such?"

"Anything I want," Blade said, studying them for a moment. "Can the two of you read?"

Maddie shook her head, while the Kid scrunched his mouth and jiggled his shoulder. "Readin' ain't important. I wouldn't mind learnin', but I don't have the time to waste."

"I don't understand," Blade said to Maddie, and nodded at the bottles, jugs, and decanters. "If you can't read the labels, how do you know the contents?"

She gazed at the shelves and grinned. "Those labels don't mean a thing. We reuse the bottles over and over again, and we fill them with whatever we want. All I have to do is remember which type is which bottle." She pointed at a squat bottle bearing a green label. "See that one there?"

"The bottle with the wine label?"

"Is that what the label says? Actually, there's vodka in that bottle."

Blade pursed his lips and lapsed into a thoughtful silence, pondering the drastic decline in culture since World War Three. The nuclear holocaust had devasted the planet, causing civilization to regress, wiping out a hundred years of progress and precipitating an era of unprecedented violence and savagery. A handful of factions scattered about the country retained some semblance of prewar living standards, but most of the U.S. had been plunged into an abyss of ignorance and barbarism. Vast tracts were virtual no-man's-lands, where mutations thrived, where slovenly conditions contributed to widespread disease, where the survival of the fittest predominated. Collectively these wild, primitive regions were known as the Outlands, and northern Wisconsin typified the deplorable quagmire into which humanity had sunk. Public education, mass transportation, medical care, and police protection were all nonexistent. Alcohol and drug use proliferated in epidemic proportions. A black market for scarce commodities thrived. Petty tyrants established dozens of city-states. The value of a human life became inconsequential.

"You've got a dandy set of pigstickers, Blade," Kid Zanto commented, intruding upon the giant's reflection.

"I like them," Blade said absently.

"I haven't seen too many Bowies in such good condition," the Kid observed. "Same for your shotgun."

"When a man's life can depend on his weapons, those weapons had better be kept in excellent shape," Blade philosophized.

"Yep," the Kid said, patting his Redhawks. "I clean my revolvers every day, whether they need the cleanin' or not."

Blade stared at the Rugers, his eyes narrowing when he spied the nine notches on each gun. "Are you keeping score?"

Kid Zanto looked at his revolvers, then beamed. "You mean the notches? Sure, I'm proud. I've worked hard to earn my rep. Everyone knows what will happen if they mess with me." He jerked his head at the closed west door through which Barney and Ed had exited lugging the bodies. "You strike me as being one mean dude. Aren't you proud of wastin' those dirtballs?"

Blade's features altered, projecting a melancholy air. "No."

"Why not?"

"Should a man measure his life by his ability to kill?"

The query confounded the Kid, whose most profound moral deliberation to date had been whether to kill a man who had insulted his sweetheart outright or to goad the man into drawing first and thus attach a minimal degree of fairness to the slaying. The Kid had opted to provoke the slime-bucket into drawing, but when his intended victim wisely refused to engage the Kid in gunplay, Zanto had shot the man in the head anyway. "I don't follow you," he said.

"Our worth lies in our capacity for love, not our capacity for destruction."

Kid Zanto cocked his head to one side and peered at the giant as he might a mutated insect. "Damn, mister. You're downright weird. Did you get those funny ideas from readin' books?"

"From books, and from the Family Elders."

"Well, old folks ain't much for smarts, if you ask me. And if books can warp your brain, I figure I'll pass on learnin' to read."

Blade sighed and gazed at Maddie. "Would you relay a message to Brount for me?"

"If you have something to say to Danny," Kid Zanto said, facing the front entrance, "you can tell him yourself. Here he is."

Gripping his shotgun, Blade pivoted and beheld four armed men entering the tavern, two of them carrying submachine guns and one bearing an assault rifle. The burly man in the lead suddenly glanced at the bar and bellowed angrily:

"You!"

CHAPTER THREE

Blade tensed, believing for a few seconds that the burly newcomer had barked at him, until he realized the leader's brown eyes were locked on Kid Zanto. As the quartet approached, threading a path among the tables, he scrutinized them. The man who must be Daniel Brount possessed a hawkish countenance with thin eyebrows, a hooked nose, and a pointed chin. His clothes, a spiffy brown suit without a tear anywhere, were in remarkable, immaculate condition. Curly brown hair crowned his head. Around his waist, visible when his coat swayed as he walked, were two Heckler and Koch P9S double-action 45's.

The three men who apparently served as Brount's personal bodyguards were a disparate bunch. The tallest, easily six and a half feet in height, resembled a massive, hulking ape. His forehead protruded two inches beyond his beady eyes, and his brows were thick and bushy. An ill-fitting green sweater and brown pants covered his powerful frame. In his hands he clutched a Colt AR-15.

The next man, slightly over six feet tall and extremely skinny, wore a baggy brown suit well past its prime. A brown fedora covered his short black hair. Cradled in his arms was an Uzi.

Trailing behind the others, his blue eyes constantly in motion, his stocky form radiating an aura of immense strength, walked a man in jeans and a green short-sleeved shirt who bore an Ingram M10. His blond hair had been clipped into a Mohawk.

"Howdy, boss!" Kid Zanto said, greeting his employer.

Daniel Brount halted a yard from the Kid and folded his arms across his chest. "Howdy? Is that all you have to say to me?"

"What more do you want?" Kid Zanto replied, mystified by the question.

"An explanation would be nice," Brount stated flatly.

"I don't get you."

Brount glanced at the bodyguard wearing the fedora. "He doesn't get me, Arnie?"

Arnie snickered.

"Perhaps I should refresh your memory," Brount said, patronizing the youth. "Do the names Barney and Ed ring a bell?"

The Kid's brow creased in concern as he abruptly perceived his boss knew about the shooting. "Barney Morris and Ed Flaunders?" he asked, stalling, racking his mind for a plausible excuse to forestall the tongue-lashing he was certain to receive.

"Don't play innocent with me, Kid," Brount said harshly. "You know damn well who I'm referring to. Imagine my surprise a couple of minutes ago when we came down Main Street and met Barney and Ed on their way to the dump, pushing a cart containing three stiffs."

"Stiffs ain't no big deal," the Kid commented.

"They are when they're killed in one of my joints," Blount declared. "Even more so when they're killed in a gunfight between customers. You know my rules on in-house gunplay. When a joint becomes known as a bad spot to hang out, the customers slack off." He paused, his voice lowering meaningfully. "I don't want to lose any customers."

"I know you don't, boss," Kid Zanto said.

"Do you? And do you know the reason I hired you as a bouncer?" Brount asked testily.

The Kid nodded. "Sure. To nip trouble in the bud was how you put it once."

"Precisely. To prevent the drunks and the troublemakers from becoming too belligerent. If anyone steps over the line, you're supposed to rein them in."

"I do a good job," Zanto remarked a shade defensively.

"Really? Barney and Ed told me they witnessed a gunfight between customers, and according to them you were nowhere around when the shooting began," Brount stated, and the next three words lashed from him like the striking of a whip. "*Where were you*?"

"Takin' a leak," Kid Zanto answered.

"Oh?" Brount said, and lowered his arms. "You wouldn't happen to be lying to me, would you, Kid?"

The youth nervously shuffled his boots.

"Because if you're lying to me, I'll fire you right here and now. I won't tolerate liars," Brount declared. "You claim you were taking a leak. I have my doubts. I suspect you were fooling around with Susie again. I know you have the hots for her, Kid. Remember when I caught the two of you together during her shift? I was lenient with you then, although I have a rule that only customers are permitted in the cubicles during work hours. But I didn't raise a stink." His tone became flinty. "But I won't be so lenient if I discover you're lying to me, so I'll give you one last chance to retract your statement. I'll ask you again. Where were you when the shooting started?"

Kid Zanto lowered his face and mumbled a response.

"I didn't quite hear you," Brount said, leaning closer.

The Kid's sheepish reply was barely audible. "With Susie, boss."

"With Susie," Brount repeated, and an indescribable rage distorted his features, arising with astounding swiftness, totally transforming his visage into a mirror of primal fury.

Blade expected Brount to hurl himself at the Kid, but instead the rage vanished as swiftly as it had appeared.

"I'm very disappointed in you, Kid," Brount said with a paternal air.

"I'm sorry," the Kid apologized, his expression a study in contrition.

The bodyguard named Arnie and the alert tough sporting the Mohawk looked at one another and smirked.

Daniel Brount cupped his hands and uttered several clicking sounds. "You've hurt me deeply, Kid. If I can't trust you, who can I trust?"

Kid Zanto's chin fell to his chest in abject humiliation. "I'm really sorry, Danny," he said softly. "You've always treated me aces. New clothes, all the booze I want, and a great job. I promise you I won't let it happen again."

"I know it won't," Brount asserted, smiling broadly. "I like you, Kid. I knew you had talent the moment I laid eyes on you at your old man's farm, when I saw you target-practicing with that pistol of your dad's. I knew you could go far if given the opportunity, and I'd hate to see anything or anyone stand in your way. You've got to learn to exercise a little self-control."

The Kid looked up, his face as eager as an adoring puppy's. "I will, Danny. You don't need to worry on that score."

"Fine," Brount said. "Fine, Kid." He patted the youth on the left shoulder. "Now back to cases. Who shot those three stiffs?"

"I did," Blade stated, intentionally grating his voice and squaring his shoulders, and he was rewarded when his psychological tactic produced the desired effect; all three bodyguards stiffened and swung toward him. Their leader, however, remained outwardly cool.

"And who might you be?" Brount asked politely, his eyes inspecting the giant from head to toe.

"Blade."

"New in Shantytown?"

"Arrived a few hours ago."

"Well, Blade, you heard everything I told the Kid. I don't like gunplay in my joints. I suppose you have a valid reason for wasting those three?"

"The best."

"What might it be?"

"They were amateurs."

To the bewilderment of Maddie, Kid Zanto, and the three bodyguards, Brount tossed back his head and laughed heartily. When he finally stopped, his eyes were twinkling. "Did they happen to have any other character flaws?"

"Yeah. They suffered from terminal stupidity."

This struck Brount as even funnier, and he vented an appreciative guffaw. "Terminal stupidity! I'll have to remember that one." He took a deep breath and another instantaneous transformation took place, an immediate sobering. "Let me explain the facts of life to you. Shantytown is my turf. I control this whole territory. Half the joints in town are owned by me, and those I don't run pay me a protection fee. Every business, every farm for miles around, pays a monthly percentage into my treasury. I have over two dozen guns working for me. In short, whatever I say goes."

Blade nodding, pretending to be suitably impressed by Brount's boasting.

"I rarely excuse unjustified gunplay in my establishments," Brount said.

Maddie choose that juncture to make a comment. "The killings were justified, Mister Brount. He protected me from those three clodhoppers."

"He did?" Brount queried. "And how many times must I tell you to call me Dan?"

Maddie ignored the request. "They were roughing me up when he came to my rescue. They left, but they came through the side door a few minutes later with their guns out, planning to kill Blade. He acted in self-defense."

Brount regarded the giant's countenance closely. "This changes everything. I won't allow my bartenders, or any of my girls for that matter, to be manhandled. You did me a favor by blowing those chumps away, and I always repay my debts. What would you like? Food and drink? Clothes? Ammo? A new gun? You name it, it's yours."

"A job."

Taken unawares by the reply, Brount straightened and blinked twice. "What?"

"I'd like a job. You must always be in the market for a new hired gun."

Brount's eyes narrowed. "Yeah. I can always use a good man. But I've never seen you in action, friend. No offense meant."

"None taken," Blade said.

"I saw him," Maddie interjected, "and I can tell you straight out that I've never seen anyone better, anyone faster."

"Is that a fact?" Brount stated, his forehead creasing as he considered the prospect. "I trust your judgment, Maddie, but I still need to see for myself."

"Put me to a test," Blade suggested.

"What kind of test?"

Blade leaned his elbow on the bar. "Any test you want." He hoped his voice projected a nonchalant attitude. The success of his strategy depended on gaining Brount's acceptance, on impressing the immoral prince of Shantytown. He expected Brount to propose a test of marksmanship, or perhaps a feat of strength.

"You're on," Brount said, and gestured at his apelike henchman. "You can fight Zed to the death."

The bodyguard so honored appeared shocked by the idea. "You can't be serious, boss."

"Never more so," Brount assured him, then looked at Blade. "Zed is as strong as any five men I know. Take him on, unarmed, and if you kill him I'll hire you."

Blade hesitated, confounded by the turn of events, by Brount's callous disdain for the bodyguard's life.

"What's the matter? Are you scared?" Brount inquired sarcastically.

Seldom had Blade slain another without provocation, and he disliked the thought of doing so now. The proposition ran counter to every ideal he cherished, to all his years of training as a Warrior. "I had no idea your men are so expendable," he mentioned offhandedly.

"If you want to work for me, you'll do what I say when I say it," Brount stated. "I have complete confidence in Zed. He's never been defeated. You have five or six inches on him, but he's got as many muscles as you do, and Zed doesn't know the meaning of the word pain. You can hit him all day, and he'll keep coming back for more. The issue here isn't expendability. The issue is a challenge for Zed, a little practice for him to keep in shape, and a test for you." He paused. "You asked for a test and this is it. Take it or leave it. But make up your mind, because I'm a busy man."

Blade knew there was no other recourse. "When and where?" he queried, wondering how long he would have to prepare.

"Right here and now."

"Now?" Blade repeated in surprise.

"Take it or leave it," Brount reiterated.

With the utmost reluctance, Blade nodded. "I accept."

A crafty grin curled Brount's mouth. "Excellent," he declared, his tone evincing excitement, and pointed at the bodyguard with the Mohawk. "Butch, clear all the tables to the sides of the room. Arnie, have all the customers belly up to the bar. Then I want both of you to haul ass and make the rounds of all the joints on Main Street. Give everybody the word. I want this place packed. Arnie, you'll handle the bets after you get back."

Butch and Arnie nodded and proceeded to accomplish their tasks.

"I thought the duel is between Zed and me," Blade noted stiffly.

"It is," Brount countered.

"Then why invite the whole town to witness the fight? Why bet on the outcome?"

"Get real, friend," Brount said. "You've given me a golden opportunity to make major money, and I'd be a fool to allow the chance to pass. We stage regular wrestling matches and prizefights, but they're not to the death. I just hope Zed doesn't finish you off too soon or the customers will be disappointed."

Blade frowned and gazed at the counter. If he wasn't so disgusted by the bout, he'd almost admire Brount's entrepreneurial enthusiasm. If he wanted, he could still decline, still walk out, but doing so entailed forsaking any possibility he had of tracing the weapons to their source. His own scheme had trapped him in an untenable position. He wavered for a full minute, until he recalled with gruesome vividness the sight of all those mutiliated innocents. Their deaths demanded justice be served.

"Do you know what you're getting yourself into?" Maddie asked anxiously.

Blade looked at her, his lips compressing.

"Damn, this is pitiful," Kid Zanto commented. "I was gettin' to like you, Blade, and now I'll have to watch Zed break you into itty-bitty pieces."

CHAPTER FOUR

A gambling frenzy seized Shantytown.

Within an hour nearly every resident knew about the impending fight to the death between the outsider, the giant who had slain three men in the Booze N' Broads and who was said to possess lightning reflexes, and Brount's bodyguard Zed, the man whose favorite means of killing a foe involved grasping his adversary's head in his immense hands and squeezing until the brains oozed out the fellow's ears. Three hundred of Shantytown's seven hundred inhabitants gathered outside the Booze N' Broads, unable to cram inside, while 72 were fortunate enough to arrive early and be admitted after paying the modest price of four bucks, the admission payable in either gold or silver ore, gold dust, gold or silver coins, jewelry, or the equivalent in barter for whatever the house deemed of value. Those in attendance could also elect to have the admission cost added to their account, to the amount they already owed Daniel Brount, and most opted to pay accordingly since they were already deeply in debt to the leading citizen, some to the tune of hundreds of dollars, and they reasoned that four more wouldn't make much of a dent in their financial status.

Patrons lined all three walls and were packed against the bar four deep. Brount had two other women brought in to assist Maddie. Arnie could scarcely keep abreast of the bets placed, while Butch and five other hired guns supervised crowd control by standing in the center of the tavern and waving their weapons at anyone who inadvertently encroached on the cleared space set aside for the contest.

Blade, Brount, Zed, and Kid Zanto stood at the west end of the bar, Brount observing the audience with a delighted grin.

"You'll make a mint, boss," the Kid remarked.

"After all the bets are tallied, I should clear ten grand, easy," Brount boasted.

"If your man wins," Blade reminded him.

"There's no doubt in my mind," Brount responded.

"Will there by any hard feelings if *I* win?" Blade asked.

"No," Brount answered, although his inflection and his expression hinted otherwise.

"You won't beat me," Zed stated. "No one has ever beaten me." He glared at Blade. "Would you like to know why?"

"Why?"

"I'm the strongest there is," Zed proclaimed with the cocky assurance a twelve-year-old might have.

Blade scanned the crowd, a ragtag bunch if ever there was one, a motley assortment of unshaven, dirty men interspersed with a score of women only a degree more fastidious in their personal hygiene and appearance. Beer and liquor flowed down their gullets in a torrent. Laughter, ribald humor, and obscenities peppered the air. There wasn't a sympathetic face in the crowd. Even those who had bet on him couldn't care less about his safety and well-being. All they craved was for him to win at any cost so they could revel in their winnings afterwards, and he would earn their undying hatred if he lost.

Arnie came over, smirking like an alley cat that had just

cornered a mouse. "The bets are all placed, boss. I gave two to one odds, just like you ordered."

"And?" Brount replied eagerly.

"I had our men spread rumors building up this bozo's rep, as you wanted."

"Get to the damn point," Brount snapped. "What's the bottom line?"

"Eleven thousand, one hundred and fifty-four," Arnie said.

"Better than I figured," Brount remarked, and rubbed his palms together. "Let's get this show on the road."

Zed placed his AR-15 on the counter, then stripped off his green sweater to expose a tremendous physique. From his neck to his waist he gave the impression of being a wall of muscle. He flexed his shoulders, grunted at Blade, and moved toward the center of the tavern while being hailed by a chorus of cheers from the throng.

"Your turn," Brount said to Blade.

The giant deposited the Mossberg and the bandoliers on the bar. He added the Bowies to the pile slowly, averse to parting with the big knives that had served him in good stead for many years and saved his life more times than he felt inclined to recall. He viewed them as a part of him, an extension of his personality and his prowess as the head Warrior. "Kid, I need a favor," he said to the youth in black.

"Hey, you name it."

"I need a man to guard my gear."

Kid Zanto's chest swelled with pride at having someone as awesome and deadly as the giant refer to him as a full-fledged man, and he nodded. "You got it. Anyone so much as breathes on your stuff, I'll plug the turkey smack between the eyes."

"Thanks," Blade said, and pivoted, his abdomen tightening. Remember the children! he told himself.

"Whenever you're ready," Brount said.

"Are there any rules?"

"Are you kidding?" Brount retorted, and snickered.

Blade advanced warily, his arms at his sides, studying his opponent.

The massive bodyguard stood in the middle of the floor, his hands on his thick hips, a contemptuous sneer directed at the Warrior. "Hurry up, jerk!" he bellowed. "I'm getting thirsty waiting for you."

His sentiments were echoed by hoots and catcalls from the audience.

"Do you prefer a particular style of combat?" Blade asked when he was within six feet of Zed.

"Say what?"

"How do you want to go about this? Karate? Savate? Kung fu? Judo? Jujitsu?"

Zed scratched his head, confused. "What the hell are you talking about? I don't know any of those things."

"I was hoping you'd say that," Blade responded.

"All I have to do is get my hands on you and you're history," Zed stated.

"Don't make me laugh," Blade said purposefully. "You couldn't beat a five-year-old at arm wrestling. The strongest thing about you is your breath. Did you eat a skunk for lunch?" The three-pronged insult provoked the intended effect.

With an inarticulate snarl of rage, his lips curling back from his yellow teeth, Zed lowered his shoulders and barreled at the giant, his arms extended to grasp the upstart about the waist.

Blade easily evaded the charge, stepping to the right and grabbing Zed's left wrist in both steely hands. He twisted and wrenched downward sharply while extending his left leg in front of the bodyguard's ankles.

To the onlookers—to those who weren't seeing two fighters too many due to the excessive alcohol in their systems, the battle seemed to be over almost before it began. One moment Zed nearly had the giant in his grasp, and the next Zed executed a spectacular somersault, unfortunately not a maneuver of his own choosing, and crashed into the wooden floor.

"That's the way, Zed!" an inebriated spectator cried in encouragement.

The bodyguard scrambled erect and faced his foe, a newfound respect penetrating his dimwitted consciousness. "You're different than most. You fight funny."

"I don't want to hurt you, Zed. Why don't you give up now and save us both a lot of effort?"

"I can't give up. Mister Brount would be mad."

"I want both of us to live," Blade stressed, raising his voice to be heard above the cheering, jeering throng.

"One of us will," Zed stated, and charged again, taking two strides and driving forward, aiming to tackle the man in the black leather vest and bring Blade crashing down where Zed could get in close. He saw his adversary spin out of the way, and he glimpsed Blade's left leg arching up and in, and then felt an intense pain in his stomach as he tumbled to the floor.

The crowd started chanting encouragement. "Go, Zed! Go, Zed!" shouted Zed's partisans, while a smaller contingent yelled for their choice to win with boisterous bellows of "Blade! Blade! Blade!"

Zed scrambled erect and crouched, cautious now, realizing a headlong rush would not bowl Blade over. He stalked forward, his fists and shoulders set in a boxing posture. "Stand still and fight like a man!" he challenged.

"As you wish," Blade said, and waded into the bodyguard with his fists flailing, blocking blow after blow while delivering a series of devastating punches to Zed's face and head.

Bloody and battered, his forearms deflecting as many blows as he could, Zed retreated slowly. He knew the stranger was clobbering him, and he knew he needed to turn the tide quickly if he wanted to win. Rock-hard knuckles connected with his chin and he staggered, and a follow-through to his stomach doubled him over. There, less than a foot away, were Blade's legs, and Zed ignored the pain in his body, ramming into his opponent and wrapping his arms around Blade's thighs.

The jarring impact rocked Blade on his heels, and before he could recover his balance, while his arms swung wildly, Zed rammed him again. Blade felt his boots leave the floor, and an instant later he came down hard, smashing onto his shoulder blades. Before he could recover, Zed's thick fingers clamped on his neck, gouging into his throat, while Zed slid upward and straddled his chest.

"Got you!" Zed hissed.

Blade grabbed his foe's wrists and heaved, striving to buck Zed off, but the bodyguard clung to him tenaciously and applied more pressure on his throat. Zed's prodigious might would crush his neck in moments unless he could dislodge those viselike fingers.

"Die!" Zed growled.

Not yet! Blade mentally resolved, and swept his legs up and around, hooking his ankles on Zed's neck and yanking his legs back and down. He succeeded in causing his opponent to sway, although Zed refused to be torn from his perch, and for a second Zed's grip slackened. Blade immediately applied all of his strength to the bodyguard's wrists, wrenching his fingers momentarily loose, then rolled to the right and heaved, flinging Zed from him.

Zed rolled with the force of the toss and sprang to his feet in a smooth motion.

Reversing his direction, Blade rolled to the left and pushed himself erect, putting a few extra feet between them in the process. His throat throbbed. He swallowed, took a breath, and adopted a horse stance.

Perturbed by the turn of events, by his inability to retain the advantage, Zed frowned and shook his head. "No one's ever broken my choke grip before."

"Do we continue?" Blade asked, his words rasping like sandpaper on metal.

For an answer, his legs pumping furiously, Zed attacked once again.

Blade crouched, his leg muscles bunching, the sinews on his arms resembling metallic cords, ready for the rush. He rated Zed as no more than a minor pawn in the organization he wanted to penetrate, and while his primary target was the man at the top, he couldn't afford to allow anyone or anything to stand in his way. He'd held back so far, influenced by a peculiar sympathy for the apish bodyguard, a sympathy now extinguished by the initial stage of their battle. If he held back any longer, if he went easy on his adversary, Zed might win by default if he became careless. So Zed must lose, and lose swiftly.

The bodyguard grinned as he closed to within a yard of the giant and went to catch Blade in a bear hug.

Only the Warrior wasn't there.

Blade ducked and rotated on the ball of his left foot, sidestepping Zed and spearing the rigid fingers of his right hand into Zed's ribs, burying them to the knuckles. The strike made Zed voice an anguished whoosh and double over, exactly as Blade wanted. He locked his right hand on Zed's throat, his left on Zed's tarnished belt buckle, and lifted, straining every fiber of his herculean physique as he raised Zed into the air, clear above his head.

Astounded by the awesome display of primal power, the spectators hushed and gaped.

Blade held his foe aloft for a full ten seconds, every muscle bulging and quivering, letting Brount appreciate the extent of his capabilities, and then he swept his arms down and heaved Zed as far as he could.

The bodyguard struck the floor eight feet off after flipping in midair, and he thudded onto his head and outflung hands, his forehead bearing the weight of his fall. He collapsed on the spot, on his knees, slumped on his left cheek, blood dribbling from a split in his forehead, his eyes closed and breathing shallowly.

The crowd responded with total silence for the space of

a heartbeat, and then a spontaneous roar of approval shook the roof.

Blade swung toward Brount and took three strides.

"Not bad," Brount said in admiration.

"Good enough for you to hire me?" Blade replied.

"You'll be hired if you kill Zed, and Zed looks very much alive to me," Brount mentioned.

"He's out cold," Blade said. "Isn't that enough?"

"Evidently not," Brount said, smirking.

"Look out!" Kid Zanto cried.

And only then did Blade realize his mistake. He'd made the cardinal blunder anyone could make while in a fight: *Never turn your back on your opponent!* He tried to whirl, too late.

Zed's right arm came around the Warrior's neck and secured Blade's throat in a strangulation grip. The arm compressed on Blade's windpipe, completely cutting off the Warrior's air, while Zed braced his left hand against Blade's back for support.

"Kill the puke!" someone shouted.

"Choke the slime-ball!" added another.

Blade grit his teeth and endeavored to pry Zed's arm from under his chin, but the bodyguard had the leverage and the upper hand and was not about to lose either. In a flash of insight, Blade perceived that his half-baked compassion might enable Zed to win!

CHAPTER FIVE

In his earlier years, before he began running all over the ravaged, post-apocalyptic countryside with various fellow Warriors, Blade had prided himself on his superb self-control. Indeed, his masterful inner discipline had gained him the trust of the Family Elders and enabled the Family Leader, Plato, to select him as the head Warrior without a single objection being lodged by an Elder. During the first half-dozen trips away from the Home to deal with threats to the Family's safety and welfare, he had maintained his self-control intact. But as more and more runs were necessitated by the appearance of addtitional dangers, he'd noticed a gradual loss of inner discipline, a budding anger at the world in general and at those power-mongers, mutations, and murderous psychopaths in particular who seemed bent on destroying any vestige of peace and stability left in the world, who wanted to plunge the remnants of civilization into a black abyss of irrevocable barbarism.

With each mission, whether as a Warrior trying to save the Family or as the head of the Freedom Force trying to preserve the Federation, he became less tolerant, less willing to give a foe the benefit of the doubt under any circumstances. Except when in the company of loved ones and friends, he seldom relaxed, and he trusted only those who had proven they were dependable and worthy of his friendship. To compound his growing cynicism, on several recent occasions he had actually lost complete control during a fight, gone totally berserk and dispatched an enemy in a frenzy of unadulterated blood lust.

And now he did so again.

As he struggled and bucked in an effort to dislodge Zed, and as each attempt met with frustration, his rage mounted, escalating until he exploded with the implacable fierceness of an erupting volcano. He tried swinging from side to side, but Zed clung on. He tried dropping to his right knee and flipping Zed over his shoulder, but Zed increased the pressure on his back and held fast. He tried reaching overhead to claw at Zed's face and hair, but Zed evaded his fingers. He tried reaching behind him to grab Zed's legs, but Zed stood as immobile as a boulder and laughed wickedly.

The laughter triggered Blade's unchecked fury.

A tremendous pain seemed to fill his entire chest when he bellowed a roar of maddened defiance with the last breath in his mouth and lumbered forward, gaining speed rapidly, heading directly toward the center of the bar, his strides lenghtening, dragging Zed after him. His face turned crimson, his veins standing out prominently.

Nonplused by this unexpected tactic, the patrons packed near the bar gawked for a second and then outdid one another in their frantic haste to get somewhere else quickly. A swirling melee ensued, a jumble of swinging limbs and gruff curses, and a space two yards wide materialized at the middle of the bar.

Blade never slowed. He ran at the counter and twisted at the very last instant, slamming Zed into the bar with enough force to crack the top. Something else cracked, and Zed's arm slipped loose. In a blur of motion, acting on an instinctive level of sheer impulse, Blade whipped his right elbow back and up, glancing over his right shoulder as he did, and he saw the tip of his elbow bash Zed on the nose. The bodyguard's nostrils flattened like so much tissue paper, and without missing a beat, continuing to move even as one blow landed, Blade arced his left elbow rearward and caught Zed on the chin.

Teeth crunched and blood spurted, and Zed staggered from the bar.

Relentlessly, without a tinge of remorse, Blade swung toward the bodyguard and rained his malletlike fists on Zed's battered countenance, hammering and hammering, heedless of the spray of crimson, the splitting of flesh, and the aching of his own hands as they contacted the heavy bones forming Zed's brow and cheeks. He hammered as Zed stumbled backwards; he hammered as Zed crumpled into a kneeling posture; he hammered until Zed pitched onto the floor with a groan and a thump.

Suddenly the red mist of rage evaporated and Blade became aware of the bloody form at his feet and the general hush in the tavern. He straightened and scanned the spectators, and on each face he beheld commingled fear and awe, with fear predominating. On Maddie he saw shock, on Kid Zanto a strange, happy smile, and on Daniel Brount a detached, calculating expression.

"I didn't think it could be done," said the latter.

Blade walked toward his gear, the customers parting from his path, wiping the gore from his hands. "Live and learn," he snapped.

"You're not done," Brount said.

"Oh?" Blade responded. He reached the pile and slid the Bowies into their sheaths.

"Zed is still alive," Brount said. "I can see his chest moving. He's still breathing."

Blade aligned the bandoliers across his chest and picked up the Mossberg. "So?"

"The deal was for me to hire you if you wasted Zed," Brount reiterated impatiently.

"Screw you and screw your test," Blade said angrily.

A collective intake of breath came from all sides.

"What?" Brount said, as if he couldn't believe his own ears.

Blade faced him. "Are you hard of hearing? Screw you and screw your test. If you want Zed wasted, do it yourself."

The bodyguard named Butch stepped from the crowd, his M10 clutched in his left hand. "Hey, asshole! Nobody talks to Mister Brount like that!"

"Who asked you?" Blade snapped, and simply angled the Mossberg barrel a few inches higher and squeezed the trigger.

Butch's forehead and Mohawk disappeared in a fountain of hair and gray matter, and the impact sent him flying four feet to crash onto his back, his legs and arms convulsing.

The abruptness of Butch's death seemed to transmogrify every person in the Booze N' Broads into a grotesque stone statue, each frozen in the act of doing whatever he or she was engaged in when the blast shattered the stillness.

Arnie and the five hired guns on the premises recovered first and converged toward the Warrior.

Blade pointed the shotgun at Brount, who flinched and took a pace backwards, and pumped in a fresh round.

"Now hold on there!" Brount exclaimed.

"If your men come any closer, you're history," Blade vowed.

Brount looked around and spied Arnie. "Don't interfere!" he ordered the man in the fedora. "Lower your weapons!"

Arnie and the others hesitated.

"Now!" Brount thundered.

Blade saw them comply and focused on the lord of Shantytown. "I've changed my mind about working for you," he declared coldly.

Brount glanced at Zed, then Butch. "I don't get it. You

could have finished Zed off easily. Why didn't you?"

"I wouldn't expect you to understand," Blade said wearily, lowering the Mossberg.

"Try me."

"Okay," Blade said, moving from the bar. "I came here because I heard you were the type of man I might be interested in working for, a man others treated with respect, and a man who treated his own people right, who paid well."

Brount listened attentively.

"Instead," Blade went on as he slowly made for the entrance, "I find a man who treats his own people like dirt, who throws their lives away on a whim. You may pay well, but you're not the type of man I want to work for." He turned and walked backwards the last 20 feet, his eyes on the hired guns.

"Wait a minute!" Brount called. "Don't be so hasty, friend."

"I'm not your friend," Blade said, and his shoulder blades touched the front door.

"We should talk some more," Brount suggested.

"No, thanks. All I want is to find a place to stay for the night, and in the morning I'll leave. I don't want any trouble." So saying, Blade reached behind him, found the doorknob, turned it, and stepped outside. He drew up short at the sight of hundreds of Shantytown residents milling about outside the tavern.

The three hundred or so loungers were awaiting the announced result of the fight. Most had wagers riding on the outcome. A few had tried to peek in the door, but one of Brount's men had sternly commanded them to keep the door shut or have their faces shot off. The boom of the shotgun had unnerved them, and they were excitedly speculating on the possible cause when the door swung out and the Warrior emerged.

"Hey, buddy!" a man with a full beard shouted upon seeing Blade. "What happened in there? Who won the fight?"

"Yeah," chimed in a young man. "Was it Zed or that other crud?"

Blade headed south on Main Street, the Mossberg cradled in his arms, passing through the crowd without hindrance. They hurriedly moved out of his path, then dozens tried to get inside the Booze N' Broads to get the scoop on the fight, pushing and shoving as too many attempted to squeeze through the doorway at once.

With over half of Shantytown's inhabitants inside or congregated outside the Booze N' Broads, the rest of the town seemed deserted. The setting sun cast a reddish glow over the uneven rows of ramshackle buildings comprising the heart of Shantytown. The structures had been improperly constructed with whatever materials the builders had found handy at the time. The walls and roofs tilted and slanted at weird angles. Doorjambs and windowsills were uneven, and most windows consisted of flaps of cloth or canvas stretched over the openings and secured with rusty nails or tacks. Sidewalks were nonexistent and none of the streets had been paved. The passage of decades and hundreds of thousands of boots or shoes had reduced the streets to wide, dusty ruts, and a recent March snowfall, since melted, had turned the dust and dirt into mud. Although a weekly garbage collection had been instituted, refuse littered the narrow alleys between buildings and reeked abominably.

Footsteps padded in the mud to his rear.

Blade whirled, his finger on the trigger.

"It's only me!" Maddie Stender blurted out, halting ten feet away, her body bundled in a faded brown coat to ward off the chill air. "Don't shoot."

"Wouldn't think of it," Blade said, smiling and lowering the Mossberg.

Maddie came forward tentatively. "I thought you might like some company."

"Is your shift over?"

"I'm off until tomorrow morning. I usually work days."

Blade resumed strolling down Main Street, and Maddie hastened to his left side.

"Where are you going?" she asked.

"Is there somewhere in this dump I can stay for the night?"

Maddie scanned the dilapidated buildings ahead. "Old Man Lewis has a hotel about three blocks from here, and he only charges four silver coins, any size, for two days and nights," she answered, and quickly continued. "But the hotel is a filthy pit. Stinks to high heaven, and there are roaches and rats all over. I doubt you'd enjoy staying there."

Blade halted and frowned. "I doubt it too."

She studied his profile in the fading light, nibbling nervously on her lower lip, and made a decision. "You can stay with me."

The Warrior looked at her quizzically. "Your family won't mind?"

"I don't have a family. No hubby, no kids, like I told you, nothing. Not even a lousy dog."

"Sounds like a lonely life to me," Blade commented.

The corners of her mouth drooped. "It wasn't always so lonely."

"What do you mean?"

"I'll explain later, maybe," Maddie said, and motioned for him to tag along, taking his acceptance for granted.

Blade wavered for a moment, then joined her. They trekked eastward along a secondary street, sloshing through the clinging mud.

"It's impossible to keep clean in Shantytown," Maddie remarked idly.

"I suppose everyone in town is waiting for the bathtub to be invented," Blade quipped.

Maddie laughed lightly. "Cleanliness isn't a high priority in Shantytown."

"They should have named this town Pigsty."

"I get the distinct impression you haven't been in many towns like Shantytown."

"I've usually bypassed towns like this to avoid trouble."

She glanced at him and grinned. "After what I saw back there, I'd say you have a sensible policy."

"Oh, I've seen run-down towns before," Blade said. "I've visited ruined cities where rats swarmed in the sewers and human rodents preyed on all travelers, and I've heard many stories about conditions in the Outlands, about how terrible life here can be, but this—this is disgusting."

Maddie peered at him intently. "Where *are* you from?"

"I can't say."

"Fine by me," Maddie said, and faced forward with a sigh. "As I started to explain earlier, Shantytown formed about the time of the war. There were a lot of refugees from the big cities flocking to this area, probably because of the lakes in this region. Maybe they just wanted to get away from possible military targets. I don't know. But I do know a small town sprang up on this spot over one hundred years ago, and Shantyhouse has been here ever since, growing a little bit every year."

"And you were born here?"

"Yes."

"Where are your parents?"

"They're dead."

"And no brothers or sisters?"

"I had one of each, but they both died."

They walked in silence for 20 yards. Blade detected a haunted aspect to her eyes and opted to bring up a new subject. "How long has Brount been running the show?"

"Eight years," Maddie said, looking at him, her inner torment evaporating. "He took over after Crusher killed Mac Volan for skimming money."

"Who's Crusher?"

"Oh. Sorry. I keep forgetting you're new to these parts. Crusher Payne controls this whole region, from Solon Springs in the north to Rice Lake to the south, and from Yellow Lake on the west to Hayward on the east. The region is divided into territories, and Brount runs this territory with Shantytown as his base of operations.''

''So Brount isn't the top man?''

''No.''

''Damn.''

Maddie stared at his agitated features. ''What's wrong?''

''Nothing,'' Blade said irritably, annoyed because now the mission would take longer than he'd anticipated, because he wouldn't return to his beloved Jenny and little Gabe as soon as he'd hoped.

''There are seven territories,'' Maddie elaborated. ''Each is about the same size. All seven lieutenants report directly to Crusher.'' She paused. ''I heard a story once, and I don't know if there's any truth to it, that a group of unionizers, I believe they were called, came to this region shortly after the war and took control. They've ruled the roost ever since.''

''Does their organization have a name?''

''The Union, though they rarely refer to the name in public. I doubt whether anyone else in Shantytown cares what they're called.''

''Where would I find Crusher?''

Maddie stopped abruptly. ''Find him? What do you mean?''

''If I wanted to look him up, where would I go?''

''Don't even think it,'' Maddie advised. ''You'd never get close to Crusher.''

''Why not?''

''His headquarters is based north of Trego. I've never been there, but I've talked to customers who have. Three dozen men guard Crusher day and night. He lives in a fancy house surrounded by mountains of dirt, and he has Monster Machines he uses to crush those who give him grief. That's how he acquired his nickname, Crusher. His real first name is Stan.''

Mountains of dirt? Monster machines? Blade wondered

if the information was accurate or merely another exaggerated tale told by men under the influence of an intoxicating beverage.

"Brount has been there lots of times," Maddie disclosed. "He won't talk about the setup, although he's let slip a few details now and then."

"Does Brount travel to the headquarters on a regular basis?"

"Yeah. The lieutenants meet with Crusher every two months. In fact, Brount is slated to attend a conference in two weeks."

This news Blade found extremely interesting. "Does he take his hired guns along?"

"A half-dozen or so."

Just then a pair of tall, lean, grimy characters approached from a nearby building, both carrying rifles.

"Hold it there, hot lips!" one bellowed.

CHAPTER SIX

Blade's nose registered the sour scent of alcohol as the pair stopped three yards off. Neither appeared particularly hostile, but he vigilantly watched their every motion, his finger caressing the trigger of the Mossberg.

"Ain't you the cutie-pie who works at the Booze N' Broads?" the thinner of the two men said to Maddie.

"What if I am?" she retorted.

"We've seen you workin'," the man said, gesturing at his partner.

"How nice," Maddie said, her tone sarcastic.

"And we think you're the prettiest girl in these parts," the man declared.

"I'm flattered," Maddie said, "and I'm also tired. Look me up at work tomorrow and I'll treat you to a drink."

"We figured we'd treat you, take you out on the town."

"I don't think so."

The man took a stride nearer and his voice hardened. "What if we insist?"

"You heard the lady," Blade interjected sternly.

Both men glared at the Warrior, glaring and hefting their rifles.

"What's it to you?" demanded the first.

"Butt out or else," stated the second.

Blade trained the shotgun on them. "Drop your rifles! Now!" he instructed them.

They balked at obeying, their intoxicated state rendering them sluggish as well as belligerent.

"I won't warn you again!" Blade promised menacingly.

The first man unwillingly tossed his rifle into the mud, scowling, and the second followed suit a second later.

"We don't want no trouble, mister," the first one said.

"Yeah, we just wanted to have some fun, is all," the second man added.

"I don't want to hear of you bothering this lady again," Blade advised them. "Start walking," he said, and pointed to the west. "Keep walking until we're out of sight, and then you can come back for your guns."

"Damned pushy people!" the thinner man muttered, moving away.

"A man can't even have a little fun anymore," opined his companion.

Blade watched them walk off, and once they were 40 yards distant he bore to the east again.

"Thanks," Maddie said.

"The least I could do."

She crossed her arms and stared glumly at the ground as she walked. "This happens all the time, and I'm sick and tired of having every lowlife in the Outlands trying to put the move on me. I want to be left alone, to live my life the way I please, not to be lusted after by every horny bastard there is."

'If you prefer to be left alone, I can find lodging elsewhere," Blade offered.

"I didn't mean—" Maddie began, and touched his right arm. "Please. I'd like you to spend the night at my place."

"Okay," he said, noting her eagerness.

They hurried to the next intersection and turned right, proceeding down a dead-end street until they came to the last structure on the left, a solitary cabin situated 20 yards from the other buildings. The cabin desperately needed repair work; the roof sagged, the porch had buckled in the center, the canvas covering the two front windows had been torn and fluttered in the breeze, and the exterior wood, once painted a light blue, was peeling and warped.

"It's not much, but I call it home," Maddie said with a trace of embarrassment.

"You deserve better living conditions," Blade commented.

"Come on," she urged, and stepped gingerly onto the porch and removed a key from her coat.

"Why bother to lock the door when anyone could climb in one of the windows?" Blade inquired.

Maddie stared at the lock, her forehead creased in contemplation. "I don't know. I never really gave the matter much thought." She inserted the key. "Contrary to what you might think, there isn't a lot of robbery in Shantytown. Brount's quite strict about thievery. Anyone caught stealing is always hanged, so there are few robberies. A lot of fights and killings, but little theft. One of the benefits of civilization, I guess," Maddie said, and chuckled.

The policy made sense to Blade. In the Outlands, where personal possessions of real value were rare except for the ubiquitous firearms, where precious personal effects were valued more highly than a human life, thievery constituted the most heinous behavior, akin to the practice in the old-time Wild West of stealing a man's horse, an act that inevitably resulted in a summary execution for the offending party. He recalled a book on the subject in the vast Family library, a book recommended by a fellow Warrior named Hickok, entitled *The Ox-Bow Incident*. The wild and rowdy Outlands, in many respects, were similar to the ancient West. If someone like Brount wanted to assert control in a lawless land, a few basic rules had to be established, the very minimum necessary to keep the lid on the turbulent populace.

"Here we are," Maddie said, opening the door and moving inside.

Blade heard shuffling from the dim interior, and within a minute the light from a kerosene lantern silhouetted Maddie as she returned to the doorway.

"Don't be shy. Come on in."

The Warrior entered to find a tidy front room, modestly furnished with a threadbare green rug, two wooden chairs, and a moth-eaten sofa patched in a dozen spots. At the rear was an open door to a bedroom, and to the right a confined cooking area.

"I had to scrimp for months to buy the sofa," Maddie remarked proudly. "It folds out into a bed."

"You have a nice home," Blade said politely.

"Who are you kidding?" Maddie responded.

"Compared to other buildings in Shantytown, your home is outstanding," he complimented her.

"Thank you," Maddie said, genuinely flattered, and removed her brown coat, revealing a Colt 380 Mustang in a holster on her right hip. She closed the door and draped the coat on a hook.

Blade nodded at the semiautomatic. "Why weren't you wearing that pistol at the tavern?"

"Brount doesn't like his female employees to wear firearms while working," Maddie replied. "He wants us to be all smiles and friendly, and he feels guns might turn the customers off. So I pack my Colt when I'm off duty." She paused. "I don't mind being unarmed at the Booze N' Broads. Normally the bouncers do a great job of protecting us. The Kid just got careless today." She pointed at the sofa. "Have a seat."

He walked over and sat down, sinking several inches into the cushion, and deposited the shotgun beside him.

"Would you care for something to drink? I have water and a few cans of battery acid."

"Battery acid?"

"Yeah. Before the war the stuff was called soda or pop. There are a lot of cans still around. A few months ago Crusher received a shipment of thirty cases found in a warehouse somewhere. Would you like a can?"

"No, thanks."

"I have a packet of crackers."

"I'm not hungry," Blade assured her, and stretched.

Maddie seated herself in the nearest chair, watching his sinews ripple and swell, admiring his handsome features.

"I appreciate you putting me up," Blade said.

"My pleasure. I don't have company often."

"You must have friends," he stated conversationally.

"A few, but they're not close, close friends. Everyone in Shantytown is too suspicious of everyone else to bare their souls, and two people can't be the best of friends unless they're willing to open up, to share their experiences, their hopes and their fears."

"Well put," Blade said.

"I had a man once—" Maddie began wistfully, and caught herself.

Blade saw the haunted aspect return to her eyes, and he cleared his throat and glanced at the kitchen area. "I might be persuaded to try a can of battery acid."

"Really?" Maddie responded, and walked to a brown cabinet in the northeast corner. She removed a red, white, and blue can and came over. "Here. They're better cold, but I don't have a stream or ice handy. The taste grows on you." She took her seat.

The Warrior took the can in his immense hand and examined the design. He found the notion of drinking from a metallic container oddly disturbing. The can reminded him of a story he'd read in a book dealing with the Romans of antiquity. The writer had cited scientific evidence to the effect the Romans had polluted themselves by drinking from lead goblets and cups. Once in their systems the lead had had a cumulative effect, tainting the Roman blood, instilling, gradually, mass paranoia, unruly dispositions, and vile degeneracy in the once-proud populace, and eventually destroying Roman culture. He also recollected information imparted by a Family Elder concerning the dental practices of the latter-day prewar Americans, who reportedly had used a variety of metal substances and alloys to fill cavities in their teeth. Documented proof later verified the fillings were having the same effect on the Americans that the lead had produced in the Romans.

"It's not poison," Maddie said jokingly, misconstruing his delay in drinking.

"You never know," Blade quipped, and inspected the can for a means to open it.

"There's a dinky tab on the top," Maddie informed him. "Just pull up on the top of the tab."

Blade gripped the gray tab and followed her directions, and succeeded in poking a finger-sized hole in the top. He raised the hole to his nose and sniffed, inhaling a sickenlingly sweet aroma.

"Try some," Maddie prompted.

He gripped the can and slowly lifted the hole to his mouth, carefully tilting the top so a trickle seeped into his mouth and down his throat. He tasted a flat, yet extremely sugary, gritty liquid and lowered the battery acid, puckering his lips in distaste.

"Do you like it?" Maddie inquired, grinning at his expression.

"Yuck. This gunk could be used to corrode nails."

"It's quite popular in Shantytown. But then, everything stemming from before the war is always popular," Maddie said. "Sometimes I think we cling to our past too much."

Blade carried the can to a counter in the kitchen and retraced his steps to the sofa. "I want to thank you again. This will do nicely for tonight," he said, patting the cushion underneath.

A slight scarlet tinged her cheeks. "There's another bed in the house."

"I couldn't take your bed."

"We could share it."

The declaration made Blade straighten, his gray eyes narrowing. "There's something you should know before we go any further."

"What?"

"I'm married."

Maddie flinched as if she'd been struck a physical blow, and she averted her face in shame. Here was the first man she'd asked to share her bed in over a year, and he'd declined. She'd had to stoke her courage to even broach the subject, and she felt strangely humiliated by his refusal.

Ever sensitive to the inner turmoil in others, Blade tried to soothe her. "I hope I haven't offended you somehow. I appreciate your offer. You're a lovely, intelligent woman, and any man would be honored to be selected as your mate. But I'm married to a wonderful woman to whom I've pledged my love and my loyalty." He paused, scrutinizing her, waiting for a reaction. "I know there are many who don't hold marriage in much esteem, who view wedlock as outdated, or as an emotional prison. They couldn't be more wrong. Our Elders teach that marriage is the ideal human union, a binding of a man and a woman in an eternal quest for spiritual harmony. I don't care whether everyone else on the planet looks down their noses at marriage. I don't care whether every other man cheats on his wife. I never have, and I never will."

She took a deep breath and looked at him. "And you claimed you're not exceptional?" she asked, mustering a smile.

"Sooner or later the right man will come along for you," Blade predicted.

"The right man came along two years ago," Maddie said sadly, her voice quavering.

Blade perceived her intense misery. "If you'd rather not talk about it . . ."

"But I do," Maddie responded quickly. "I need to tell

someone. I need to get the burden off my chest, and you're the only person in Shantytown I can trust.''

The Warrior settled back and waited, watching her closely.

''A little over two years ago a man arrived in Shantytown, a newcomer from the East. He started a farm seven miles from here, and the farm prospered because he was smart and strong, a big, powerful man, a lot like you, only he didn't have nearly as many muscles. At the time I was working at the Booze N' Broads and had been there for less than a year. The newcomer, Vernon Feldman was his name, started to flatter me with a lot of attention. Although I had a standing policy not to date customers, Vern melted my resistance and we began seeing each other regularly. Before long, we were constantly together. He told me his plans for his farm, and about his hopes to raise a large family, and he brought up the subject of marriage more than once,'' Maddie detailed, and stopped.

Blade knew her tale would end in tragedy, so he wisely held his counsel.

''I should back up a bit and explain the circumstances of my working for Brount. You see, any woman in Shantytown would give anything to work for Brount. Most of them, anyway. Brount runs basically clean joints, far better than the other dives. The working conditions aren't as severe, and he pays slightly more than the other business owners. Whenever a position opens, Brount can pretty much take his pick from dozens of women,'' Maddie said, and paused. ''I never even applied for the bartending job at the Booze N' Broads. Brount came to me three years ago, claming he'd heard I needed a job, and claiming he'd like to help.'' She snorted at the memory.

Blade absently shifted the shotgun to his lap.

''The scumbag wanted to help, all right. Help himself to me! He knew my father had died a month before he knocked on my door, and he knew my mom, brother, and sister were already dead. My mother passed on when I was fifteen. She contracted pneumonia. My sister was killed four years ago by a mutate while out picking berries, and my brother was murdered by a drunk less than six months later. After our sister died, he started hanging out until all hours, drinking and gambling, and one night he got into a fight over cards and lost."

The Warrior frowned, conducting mental calculations, realizing Maddie had lost her sister, brother, and father all within the span of a year.

"Anyway, when Vern came along I was all alone. I'd been working for Brount for a year. In all that time he'd treated me with respect. Never once tried to take advantage of me, but I suspected he was after me. He always played the part of a gentleman. Why he didn't just rape me, I'll never know. Rape is common in the Outlands. I think he viewed me as someone special. And while he was being so kind to me, and I was under his protection, no one else dared come close. Other men left me alone. All except for Vern."

A faint noise from outside made Blade tense and listen.

"Vern didn't know any better," Maddie said, smiling. "He definitely wasn't scared of Brount. Neither was I, but I'd heard rumors about Brount. I knew what he was capable of, and I failed to warn Vern. Part of the blame for what happened to him is mine."

The noise was repeated, and Blade casually tilted his head toward the front door.

"For eight glorious months Vern and I were madly in love," Maddie was saying, oblivious to all else except her remembrance. "Then the trouble began. Vern received death threats, advising him to leave the region or else. His equipment was destroyed. His livestock was killed. He tried to discover the identities of those responsible. We knew there were more than one involved, because often they would leave their tracks in the mud. No one would aid us. No one knew a damn thing. Vern's acquaintances shied away from him. He was left all alone." Sorrow lined her eyes.

Without appearing to be alarmed, Blade took hold of the Mossberg with his right hand.

"I was frantic. I guessed that Brount was behind the threats and the destruction of Vern's property, but I couldn't prove a thing. I pleaded with Vern, begged him to forget the farm and leave this area and take me with him, but he wouldn't listen," Maddie said, lowering her eyes to the floor. "He refused to be run off the place. The farm was ours, he said, the home for our future children, the home where we would spend many delightful years together. He had all these great plans for expansion, for adding rooms for the kids, and for little things like hanging a swing on a tree." She looked at the Warrior. "I loved that man more than life itself."

Blade nodded and casually inspected the shotgun.

"For three months the harassment continued, and then it suddenly stopped. For no reason the farm was left alone. We didn't know what to make of it at first, and Vern finally decided that whoever had been giving him the hard time had called it quits, had figured there was no way to scare Vern off. Vern believed we'd be safe from then on."

Blade adjusted his bandoliers.

"But it was all too good to be true, just the calm before the storm," Maddie said bitterly. "For two weeks everything was great, and then one day I was working bar and in came a runner saying Vern had been hurt out at the farm. Brount gave me the rest of the day off, and I borrowed a horse and rode out to Vern's." She paused and groaned.

The Warrior gazed at the door.

"I didn't get there in time. Vern was dead when I arrived. His body, especially his face and shoulders, had been beaten and whipped down to the bone. A neighbor found Vern lying in a ditch bordering Vern's farm and took him to the farmhouse, then sent for me. The guilty parties were never found. Scavengers, everyone said, but I knew better. Brount had Vern killed! Brount! And if it's the last thing I ever do, I'll prove Brount was behind Vern's murder. Why do you think I've stayed on at the Booze N' Broads? Somehow, someway,

I'll make Daniel Brount pay. I don't know what I can do against him and all his guns, but—" Maddie froze when she saw Blade raise his left hand for silence.

The next instant the Warrior bounded from the sofa to the front door, leveled the Mossberg, and wrenched the door wide open.

CHAPTER SEVEN

One moment Maddie was on the verge of bursting into tears, and the next she erupted in laughter.

There stood Brount's top gunman, Kid Zanto, with his arms outstretched and his fingers spread, leaning forward from the hips, his head twisted sideways, caught in the act of eavesdropping with his left ear pressed to the door, his stunned visage a study in amazement. The door had been pulled inward so abruptly, he was caught dead to rights. To compound his predicament, Blade's shotgun lightly touched the Kid's left cheek.

"Were you inspecting the door for termites?" the Warrior quipped.

"Brount sent me," Kid Zanto blurted out.

Blade gouged the barrel into the youth's cheek. "Why? To try and finish the job Zed started?" he demanded angrily.

"No! Nothin' like that," the Kid declared. "Look, this is humiliatin'. Can I straighten up?"

"Only if you do so slowly. One move toward those Redhawks and you'll lose your head."

"Believe me, I ain't crazy," the Kid said, straightening

but keeping his arms outstretched. "I've seen what you can do, remember? Besides which, I sort of like you, mister. You play square, and I admire a man who plays square."

The Warrior regarded the gunman for a full minute, until Zanto fidgeted uncomfortably, and then lowered the Mossberg. "Something tells me I can still trust you, but I won't tolerate being spied on by you or anyone else."

"I just was wonderin' what you two were up to," the Kid said with a wink, and smirked.

"I also won't tolerate anyone insulting Maddie," Blade announced. "She's my *friend*, and anyone who insults her will eat their teeth for their next meal at my expense. Understand?"

"Simmer down. I understand," Kid Zanto said. He noticed Maddie staring at the giant in a strange manner.

"Now what's this about Brount?" Blade inquired.

"Brount wants you to stop by the Booze N' Broads in the morning. He wants to hire you real bad."

"Maybe I don't want to work for him."

The Kid hooked his thumbs in his gunbelt and grinned. "I'm not about to tell you what to do, but you should at least go talk to the man. What harm can it do?"

Blade didn't respond.

"Man, you are the talk of the town. First you wasted those three chumps, then you beat Zed, and to top it all off you blew Butch away. Everyone in Shantytown is flappin' their gums about you."

"How is Brount reacting?" Maddie interjected.

"Better than I would've expected," the Kid answered. "He didn't raise a stink over Butch dyin', and he cancelled all the bets."

"He what?" Maddie repeated in surprise.

Kid Zanto nodded. "Shocked my shorts too. First time I ever saw him call all the bets off. He made an announcement to everybody at the joint. Since the fight was supposed to be to the death, and since Blade and Zed both survived, then Brount declared all the bets were invalid. Null and void were his words."

"Will wonders never cease," Maddie muttered.

The Kid eyed Blade. "You made quite an impression on Mister Brount. He was flattered you wanted to work for him. After what you did, he'll make you a terrific offer."

"But I spared Zed," Blade observed.

"Now there's a funny thing," Kid Zanto said. "I expected Danny to be ticked off at you for not killin' Zed, but he wasn't. In fact, I heard him tell Arnie that the fact you hadn't killed Zed proved you could be trusted, proved there's a line you won't cross over, not for anybody but yourself." He paused and scratched his chin. "Didn't quite make sense to me."

Maddie moved nearer to the doorway, gazing at Blade's profile. "What will you do?"

Before the giant could answer, from the darkness beyond came two low clicking noises.

The next transpired so swiftly, Maddie stood rooted to the spot in the seconds it transpired. She saw Blade and Kid Zanto both stiffen, both moving as they did, Blade out the door a stride to the left, the Kid whirling to the right with his back to the cabin, his hands flashing to those Ruger Redhawks, and even as the two men moved, in the blink of an eye a pair of rifle shots blasted from the night, flaming red and orange points of light, but so incredibly fast were Blade and the Kid that they returned fire at nearly the same second they were fired upon, Blade pumping the Mossberg twice, Kid Zanto's big revolvers booming four times.

And then silence.

Maddie felt a soft breeze on her cheeks, and she stared at a bullet hole in the left jamb, then over her left shoulder at a hole in the bedroom wall. The round had passed through the doorway, narrowly missed her shoulder, and smacked into the wall to her rear. She shuddered when she realized she'd been within inches of dying.

"Stay here," Blade ordered, and dashed from the cabin, the Kid staying on his right, both of them stooped over to minimize their silhouettes against the cabin doorway.

"There!" the Kid declared.

Blade saw them, a pair of forms sprawled practically side by side, a pair of tall, lean, grimy characters whose rifles were lying nearby. In the dim light, stark and gruesome, the ragged hole in the chest of the man Blade had hit was discernible.

Kid Zanto leaned over to peer at their faces. "I didn't know these two," he said in disgust, and kicked the man he'd slain. "They must've been tryin' to boost their reps."

"I knew them," Blade said.

The Kid glanced at the Warrior. "You did?"

"Yeah. Maddie and I bumped into them earlier."

"Friends of yours?"

"They gave us a hard time. They were drunk," Blade explained.

The Kid gazed at the corpses. "Yeah, well, I couldn't help but notice that folks who bump into you and give you a hard time have this nasty habit of keelin' over and dyin'. Do you suppose there's any connection?" he asked, grinning.

"I treat everyone with respect, and I require that they treat me with the same respect. If they don't, they experience the consequences."

Kid Zanto chuckled. "It's nice to see you don't go overboard with that love business you were talkin' about."

The innocent comment made Blade do a double take, and he looked down at the bodies in consternation.

"Well, I'll go get a detail to cart these dirtballs off," the Kid offered. "We can't leave stiffs on the streets. Attracts too many rats and sometimes a mutant." He pivoted, about to leave.

"Kid?"

The youth halted. "Yeah?"

"Why do you work for Brount?"

"What a weird question. Danny is tops."

"He lets you call him Danny?"

"Of course. We're the best of buddies. He's taken me

under his wing and is teachin' me all the ropes. Someday I'll move up in the organization, just like him,'' the Kid stated.

''How long have you worked for him?'' Blade probed.

''What's with all the questions?'' Zanto responded. ''About two years. He took me on right after my dad died.''

Blade's features were shrouded in shadows. ''Did your dad want you to work for Brount?''

''No, Dad was dead set against the notion,'' the Kid said, his tone softening at the mention of his father. ''Dad wanted me to be a farmer like him. I used to practice with Dad's pistol every chance I got, and Danny saw me a few times when he came to the farm to pick up a load of brew. He asked me to work for him, and I might've said yes right away if not for Dad.''

''What happened to your father?''

The Kid's slim shoulders slumped. ''He died. Had an accident.''

''What kind of accident?''

''I'd rather not talk about it.''

Blade looked at the youth. ''Please. I know it's hard. Humor me.''

Kid Zanto shrugged. ''For you I will. We had a two-story barn with a hayloft in the top, and my dad was loadin' bales into the loft usin' a winch and a rope. Dad had done the chore hundreds of times. He could do the job in his sleep. But something went wrong. He got his neck tangled in the rope, and the weight of the bale on the other end hanged him.'' The Kid paused. ''He strangled to death. What a horrible way to go.''

''Where were you when it happened?''

''Takin' a wagonload of brew into Shantytown. Brount's boys were supposed to pick it up themselves, but Danny sent word his wagon was broken so I did the job myself. He paid me extra,'' the Kid detailed.

''Nice man,'' Blade said flatly.

"Danny's tops," the Kid reiterated. "Is there anything else you want to know?"

"No. Thanks."

"Be back in a bit," the Kid said, walking into the night.

Blade spun and stalked toward the cabin, clenching the Mossberg so tightly his knuckles were white, in the throes of a personal upheaval.

Maddie took one look and recoiled, stepping backwards to allow him to enter. "What's wrong?" she queried anxiously.

The Warrior halted in the doorway, his countenance radiating rage. "Do you intend to continue working at the Booze N' Broads?" he asked gruffly.

"Of course. I need to put food on the table."

"What if I bought food for you?"

"I can provide for myself, thank you. And I'm not quitting until I prove Brount killed Vern. I want that bastard dead!"

Blade stepped inside. "You'll have to wait your turn."

"What happened out there?"

The Warrior moved closer, looming above her. He ignored her question and addressed her, lowering his voice. "I can't reveal the reason I came to Shantytown yet, but I will tell you this much. I despise Brount as much as you do. Before I leave, Brount and everyone who works for him will be dead or will be heading for parts unknown. The same holds for Crusher Payne."

"You plan to take *all* of them on?"

"I was sent here to accomplish a mission, and a Warrior always achieves the mission or dies trying."

"A Warrior? You say the word like it's a title."

"It is."

Maddie's forehead furrowed and she bit her lower lip. "I seem to recall hearing a story about a Warrior or Warriors, but what was it?"

"Never mind. All you need to know is I'm on your side, and I intend to insure Daniel Brount and Crusher Payne get what they deserve.''

The intensity of his passion disturbed her, and Maddie placed her right hand on his huge shoulder. ''Hey, friend, as much as I want to see Brount six feet under, as much as I hate his guts, I don't let my feelings get the better of me like they've done to you. You sound as if you're torn up inside.''

''I am.''

''Over Brount?''

''No, over more than Brount.''

''Care to explain?'' Maddie asked, her curiosity aroused anew.

Blade sighed and turned, stepping to the door and gazing into the darkness. ''I wouldn't know where to begin.''

''Try me.''

''You mentioned the state of the world earlier. You talked about the mutations, the radioactive toxins, and all the chemical poisons in the environment,'' Blade said, his words barely audible. ''I've seen it all, Maddie. I've traveled to every corner of the country once known as the United States of America. I've been to Canada and to the former state of Alaska.''

''And?'' she prompted when he stopped.

''And I've seen monstrosities that would give you nightmares, abominations of nature that would shred the flesh from your body and devour you in a gulp. I've met madmen, lunatics, and power-mongers, intent on compelling others to conform to their demented will or doctrines. I've lost track of the number of innocent people I've seen killed, by every brutal and savage method you can imagine, atrocities no one should have to see.''

''I can imagine,'' Maddie confirmed.

''Late last year I came to the decision to take time off from my work, to devote time to my Family and to my wife and son. I wanted to forget all the killing and the violence. I wanted to put all that behind me for a while.''

''You wanted to start over with a clean slate?''

Blade shook his head and swiveled his neck, relieving a kink. "Not exactly. In my line of work a clean slate isn't possible, not unless I live long enough to become an Elder. No, I simply wanted a breather, a break from the grind. I'd hoped to take a full year off."

"What happened?" Maddie queried.

"What always happens? Another threat arose and they needed someone to deal with it."

"Who are they?"

"I can't say," Blade reminded her.

"Sorry. I won't pry."

"Anyway, the point of all this is that I'm sick and tired of encountering scum like Brount and Payne, sons of bitches who trample all over anyone who stands in their way. I wish we could remove all of them with a snap of our fingers."

"Bastards like Brount and Crusher Payne won't vanish with a snap of the finger. If their type is to disappear off the face of the earth, then whenever one of their type puts in an appearance, someone else who is tougher and stronger, someone who believes in all the basic, decent values Brount and Crusher despise, must come along and stomp them into the dirt," Maddie stated.

The Warrior managed a grin and looked down at his feet. "Is that why I can't seem to keep my combat boots clean?" he quipped, and straightened. "The way this mission is shaping up, I'll need a new pair soon."

CHAPTER EIGHT

A profound change had settled upon the residents of Shantytown. Whereas on the day of the Warrior's arrival hardly anyone gave him more than a second glance because of his towering size, now everyone, absolutely everyone, gave him the widest possible berth. Hardened men, men who had lived their entire lives in the tumultuous Outlands, killers and ruffians and bruisers of the worst sort, went out of their way to avoid passing too near to his person. He was easy to spot, and they would cross the street a block from him to give the impression they were keenly interested in the store or bar window on the other side. Mothers with their children would scamper from his path. Once, as he passed an alley, a drunk stumbled from the depths and accidentally collided with his right arm.

"Who the hell?" the drunk had demanded, and looked up.

Seldom had Blade beheld such a comical expression as the one the drunk had then adopted. The drunk's fainting had been the icing on the cake.

But the incident with the drunk had occurred three blocks ago, and there, in sight ahead, was the Booze N' Broads.

Blade halted, noting the seven horses waiting outside. Newcomers or some of Brount's men? The morning sun afforded scant warmth for his skin as he strolled to the entrance, the Mossberg in his right hand, then opened the door.

Muted voices fell silent at the Warrior's entrance. The usual crowd, the daily regulars, had not yet arrived. A woman with black hair tended bar. Brount, Kid Zanto, Arnie, and three hired guns were leaning against the counter. All of them had swiveled toward the door as it opened. Daniel Brount beamed broadly and advanced across the room.

"Blade! You came!"

The Warrior deliberately made his features inscrutable and walked forward warily. "The Kid said you wanted to see me."

"I have a proposition for you," Brount said, halting and gesturing at the bar. "Come and join me in a drink while we discuss business."

"I don't drink."

"You don't!" Brount exclaimed, and smiled. "All the better. Gunmen who drink always cause trouble sooner or later."

"Why did you send Zanto? Do you want to conduct another test?" Blade asked sarcastically.

Brount's eyes narrowed. "You never let up, do you, friend? No, I'm not stupid enough to try and put you through another test. I asked you to come because I want you to work for me."

"We've been all through this. I didn't kill Zed like you wanted, remember?"

"Screw Zed. I don't care about that. I want you to work for me anyway."

"Why?" Blade inquired. "Do you like my cheerful personality?"

Brount laughed uproariously. "I'll come right out with my reason, just to show you I'm being honest with you. Shantytown is my turf, but from time to time upstarts pop up who think they'd like to take over, or I have a financial disagreement with one of my suppliers, or a wild bunch blows into town and tries wrecking one of my joints. There's always something," he complained.

"You have my sympathy," Blade said dryly.

"Obviously, I need to hire men who can take care of themselves, who are better than those they go up against. The better my men are, the less headaches I get. Some of my boys acquire feared reputations, and that's all for the better. A reputation works in my favor. Take the Kid, for instance. He's had to kill ten men in two years, and the word of mouth has been tremendous. If a stranger blows into town, one of the first stories he'll hear is about Kid Zanto. The Kid with the lightning hands, they call him. Very few men, no matter how tough they think they are, will want to buck me and risk going up against the Kid."

"Fear keeps everyone in line."

"Exactly. You're off to a flying start already. Five men killed in one day and Zed beaten to a pulp. You're deadly with that shotgun, your fists, and, I'd wager, even deadlier with those knives. You're perfect for a man like me, which is why I'm willing to pay you four times the going rate," Brount said, his voice lowering. "You'll even make more each month than the Kid. He's forgetful sometimes, and I need a mature man I can rely on."

"I don't know," Blade said, feigning disinterest.

"Where else will you get a cherry deal like this?" Brount responded. "I'll cover any expenses you run up and add them to your salary. Here. Look at this." He reached into his right front pocket and extracted a brown leather pouch that jingled when he extended his arm. "This is for your first month, up front."

Blade took the pouch, surprised at the weight. He undid a leather cord at the top and peered inside to discover over a dozen coins, eight of them gold, the rest silver. He whistled appreciatively, as if the money impressed him.

"See what I mean?" Brount said, pleased with himself, believing his eloquent powers of persuasion had prevailed.

"Once a month I'll receive this much?"

"That's right."

"You must be filthy rich," Blade commented.

Brount took the statement as a personal compliment. "I'm set for life, if that's what you mean. You can be too, if you play your cards right. The organization I work for pays very well. It's been in business for a century, maybe longer. You wouldn't believe how much wealth can be amassed in ten decades."

"I might believe it."

"We'll buy anything of value for a pittance or trade at a profit, so we always come out ahead. The winnings from our gambling tables are even more substantial. Four of those horses outside were taken from a guy who lost his shirt at poker."

"I saw the horses," Blade remarked.

"Speaking of which, we have a job to do," Brount said, and stared at the Warrior. "What will it be? Are you working for me or not?"

Blade closed the pouch and slid the payment into his left front pocket. "You've hired yourself another gun."

"I knew I would," Brount boasted, then headed for the entrance with a wave of his right arm.

"What's up?" Blade asked. He saw the Kid, Arnie, and the others following.

"I'm having one of those disagreements with a supplier," Brount said as he led the Warrior outside. "The man is trying to cheat me. I've tried to be patient with him, to reason with him, but he refuses to listen to reason. So we're riding out to his farm today to resolve the issue." He pointed at a big roan. "There's your animal. I didn't think to ask, but you know how to ride, don't you?"

"I can ride."

Kid Zanto, Arnie, and the hired guns came through the

door.

"Mornin', Blade," the Kid said with a smile.

"Morning," Blade replied, noting that Arnie and the three goons all carried automatic or semiautomatic weapons. Resolving the issue, evidently, did not involve dialogue.

"Mount up," Brount barked.

The Warrior swung onto the roan, shifting the Mossberg into his left hand and holding the reins in his right. He allowed Brount to lead the others north on Main Street and brought up the rear, where he could keep an eye on the paid assassins and avoid being shot in the back. He accepted Brount's offer as genuine, but he still didn't trust the man, and he definitely didn't trust Arnie. He'd received the impression Arnie and Butch were close friends, and Arnie might hold a grudge. In any event, he felt safer at the rear.

Kid Zanto drifted back to ride alongside the Warrior. "I was hopin' you'd take the job. I'm lookin' forward to workin' together."

"Where are we going?" Blade asked.

"Out to Neblette's place, about five miles northwest of town," the Kid said. "Neblette has a son not much older than me, and they're both scrappy. If push comes to shove, they'll fight."

"How are they trying to cheat Brount?"

"Danny didn't say. Who cares? They'll step into line or else."

"You're very loyal to Brount," Blade mentioned.

"Danny has taken good care of me since my dad died. Why shouldn't I be loyal to him?" the Kid replied.

"Because of your father," Blade said softly, confident the hired killers riding eight yards in front of him couldn't overhear his remark.

"What do you mean?" Kid Zanto queried, perplexed.

"You'll understand when the time comes."

"Are you sayin' I shouldn't be loyal to Danny because my dad wasn't very fond of him?"

"No."

"Then what?" the Kid pressed the issue.

Blade looked the youth in the eyes. "When the time comes," he reiterated. "You'll have to trust me until then."

"I ain't much for trustin' folks too far."

"Give me a couple of weeks," Blade said. "You'll understand eventually."

The Kid reluctantly dropped the subject, but his intent aspect indicated he was absorbed in thought.

They left the town far behind, staying on the barren, muddy track constituting a road, passing pedestrians frequently, and occasionally encountering other riders or a farm family in a wagon.

Blade wondered about the absence of vehicles. He knew cars and trucks were scarce in the Outlands, what with fuel and spare parts being so difficult to obtain, and had seen only horses and wagons since coming to Shantytown. But prior experience had taught him to expect at least one or two dilapidated vehicles in an urban center the size of the town. Considering Brount's wealth and ego, Blade would have expected the man to own a vehicle. Yet there were none in Shantytown. Why? He posed the question to the Kid.

"Crusher gets all the vehicles, all the spare parts."

"Why?"

"You're a bundle of questions, you know that? Crusher uses eight or nine cars and trucks, and those three Monster Machines of his, to protect and patrol the gravel pit."

"The what?"

Kid Zanto sighed. "Down near Trego. You'll see for yourself if Danny takes you to the next big meeting."

"I hope he does."

The road wound into a series of low hills, and the countryside on both sides became heavily forested. Animal noises emanated from the vegetation, intermixed with noises difficult to identify, intermittent screechings and wailings. Brount and his men scanned the trees vigilantly.

"There are mutants in these woods," the Kid told Blade. "They usually don't bother folks travelin' on the road in broad daylight, but you can never tell."

They continued uneventfully until they came to a wide valley and took a fork to the left, bearing westward. A red farmhouse and barn appeared, the barn to the right with a wagon parked near the southeast corner. Three horses stood in a corral to the left.

"Neblette's place," Kid Zanto informed the Warrior.

Blade saw an elderly woman emerging from the farmhouse, wiping her hands on her white apron. She moved along a stone walk to the flat area in front of the barn and awaited them.

"She's Neblette's squeeze," the Kid mentioned, and yawned.

The woman's face betrayed her mounting apprehension. She smoothed the apron and clasped her hands in front of her waist.

"Hello, Nancy!" Brount hailed her, and reined up ten feet distant. "How are you?"

"What are you doing here, Daniel Brount?" she answered.

"Why, Nancy, you sound angry at me," Brount said good-naturedly, leaning down to pat his mount.

"I won't have you making trouble for my husband," she stated harshly.

"I pay you a friendly visit, and you automatically assume I'm here to make trouble. I'm hurt," Brount said, smiling hugely.

"I want you and your thugs to get off our property," Nancy Neblette snapped. "Right this instant."

"No can do, Nancy."

"Please!" she beseeched him, taking a pace nearer. "Leave Ted alone!"

"I came all the way out here to settle our differences, and I'm not leaving until we do," Brount said.

"You'll leave right now, you son of a bitch!" thundered a new voice from the right.

Blade twisted in the saddle to find an elderly man standing near the wagon, a double-barreled shotgun gripped in his steady, callused hands and trained on Brount. A movement in the barn drew his attention, and Blade spotted a younger man, evidently Neblette's son, armed with a rifle and standing just inside the wide barn door.

"Whoa, there, Ted!" Brount called, turning his horse so he could confront the farmer directly. "Don't be hasty."

"I'll blow your damned head off if you don't get off my farm," Neblette warned.

"I came here to talk," Brount said.

"Like hell you did. We've done all our talking. I'm not about to stop supplying a few friends with brew just because you're so damned greedy you want all the business!"

"Greed isn't the issue here."

"Your ass!" Neblette spat.

"Listen to me, Ted. I've explained this a dozen times already, but I'll give you one more chance to see the light. I'm in the business of furnishing drinks to thirsty customers, and you're in the business of farming and supplying me with home brew to serve in my joints. You're one of many who supply me, and my rules for them have to apply to you too. I can't make any exceptions. And one of my rules is that no one, positively no one, sells brew or shine on the side. Anyone who wants to buy either can buy it from me."

"The hell you say," Neblette snapped. "I've been selling kegs to a few buddies of mine for years, and I'm not about to stop now."

"I didn't learn of your sales until two months ago, and I've given you more than enough time to agree to quit."

"What's the big deal?" Neblette responded. "You know I'm not making any money off the deals. I sell to my buddies at cost."

"Money or profit isn't the issue here either," Brount said. "How many times must I explain this to you? It's a matter of prestige, of reputation. I can't allow anyone, no matter how long they've been supplying me or how much I might like them, to undermine my authority. All you have to do, right now, is promise to stop supplying your friends and I'll forget the whole thing."

"Ted, please!" the farmer's wife interjected. "We can't buck *him*!"

Neblette pondered the issue for over a minute, gazing from Brount to his wife and back again. Finally he shook his head. "I gave my word to my buddies years ago, and I'm not about to go back on my word now."

Brount studied the reins in his right hand. "Is that your final word?"

"I'm afraid it is," Neblette declared.

Clucking softly, Brount guided his horse a few yards from his men, putting himself out of the line of fire. He deliberately looked at Blade. "No one can accuse me of being unfair, or of not being a patient man. But there is a limit to my patience," he said, as if justifying his motives. He then glanced at Arnie and uttered two words with chilling indifference:

"Kill them."

CHAPTER NINE

In the instant before Daniel Brount gave the order to exterminate the Neblette family, Blade deduced Brount's intent. He guessed what was coming and reacted accordingly, bringing up his Mossberg, intending to down Arnie and the three other killers, knowing full well he could never allow innocent farmers to be butchered while he sat by and did nothing. He also knew slaying the paid guns would seriously endanger his mission, but his concern for the welfare of the Neblette family overrode his better judgment. Unfortunately for the Neblettes, at the very moment Blade was about to shoot the nearest assassin, Ted Neblette cut loose with one of the barrels on his double-barreled shotgun, the blast hurling a lean assassin from the saddle and causing the other horses to rear and plunge. Blade had to grab the reins with both hands, the Mossberg clamped tightly in three fingers, in order to stay on board.

Neblette roared and charged, firing the second barrel, striking a second killer in the chest and toppling the man to the ground. He frantically broke the shotgun open and tried to reload as his son provided covering fire from the barn.

The farmer's wife screamed.

Arnie pointed his Uzi at Neblette and squeezed his trigger, and a pattern of red dots erupted across the farmer's chest. Neblette staggered backwards and collapsed.

Out of the barn came the son, furiously working the rifle, and he succeeded in slaying the third hired gun, then sighted on Brount.

Still struggling to control the roan, Blade glimpsed the Kid drawing and firing three times, incredibly quick, *bam-bam-bam*, and Neblette's son was slammed to the hard earth. Blade heard the Uzi chatter a millisecond later, and he assumed Arnie had fired at the son. Only when the roan had quieted and Blade surveyed the blood bath did he see Nancy Neblette lying on her right side, a pool of crimson forming around her, cut in half by the Uzi.

"Well, that's that," Brount said casually seconds later, nudging his horse over to the farmer's body. "You were a fool, Ted," he said to the corpse.

"What about the farm, boss?" Arnie asked, slapping a fresh magazine into his Uzi.

"The usual," Brount answered absently. "Auction the farm off to someone we can trust. And send a burial detail out here to dispose of these bozos before the animals get to them."

"As soon as we get back," Arnie promised.

Brount rode over to the Warrior. "Sorry about the roan. I forgot to tell you it's a bit skittish around gunfire. My mistake, and I apologize."

"No harm done," Blade said lamely, doubting Brount's sincerity. He observed the Kid staring at Nancy Neblette.

"There was no call to kill her," Zanto declared.

"She must have been caught in the cross fire," Brount stated apologetically.

"The hell she was," the Kid snapped. "Arnie gunned her down. I saw him out of the corner of my eye."

"Is that true, Arnie?" Brount inquired innocently.

The man in the fedora grinned. "I had to shoot her, Mister

Brount. I saw her reaching under her apron and figured she was going for a weapon."

"Let's check," Brount said, and slipped to the ground. He walked over to Nancy Neblette and knelt, his back to the men on horseback. "Well, look at this!" he exclaimed, and straightened with a revolver in his left hand, a Smith and Wesson Model 64 sporting a two-inch barrel.

"I told you," Arnie said.

The Kid stared at the Smith and Wesson, distraught. "I never would've expected her to pack a hideout gun."

"You never can tell," Brount said, sticking the gun in his left pants pocket and returning to his horse. "Do you know what your problem is, Kid?" he asked as he climbed into the saddle.

"What, Danny?" the Kid replied sheepishly.

"You're too damned trusting for your own good. Never give anyone the benefit of the doubt."

Kid Zanto, his brow knit in uncharacteristic reflection, stared at his employer. "No one, huh?"

"No one," Brount reiterated. "Everyone is out to nail you, and you have to look out for number one."

"My dad wasn't out to nail me."

Brount seemed startled by the comment. "I didn't mean your dad, of course. He was the salt of the earth. What in the world made you bring him up anyway?"

"Oh, nothin'. Just thinkin', I guess."

"There's no comparison between good men like your father and bastards like Neblette," Brount stated, and started to ride off.

Kid Zanto looked at the farmhouse, the barn, and the bodies of Nancy and Ted Neblette. "None at all," he echoed hollowly, and wheeled his horse.

Once again Blade stayed at the rear, his agitated mind awhirl, pondering the events. His inability to save the Neblettes gnawed at him, and he kept seeing Nancy Neblette, crumpled and bloody, in his mind's eye. The Kid's attitude sparked him with a flicker of hope. An ally with Zanto's ability would be invaluable in the clinches, and he hoped he could persuade the Kid to see the light before Brount departed to attend the next meeting at Crusher Payne's. Engrossed in his musing, Blade lagged behind the others. Twenty yards separated them from him when he heard the low growl.

They were passing through the forest. Without their foliage, with few in bloom so early in the year, the trees reared skyward like spiked, accusing fingers, as if they were cursing the heavens for the polluted soil in which they had to grow, for the radioactive agents that had caused many of the trees to become deformed or stunted, and for the defiled atmosphere they had to breathe.

The Warrior's head snapped up at the sound of the growl, and he glanced to the right and left, searching the woods for the source.

Another growl made the horse whinny.

Blade pinpointed a large, dark form crouched at the base of a tree ten feet to his right. He shifted in the saddle, beginning to bring the Mossberg around, hoping the creature wouldn't attack.

It did.

With a guttural snarl the beast flew at the roan, its front paws slashing. Whether its ancestors had come from wolves or from a pack of feral dogs was immaterial. All that mattered to the Warrior was the ravenous, gross mutation endeavoring to disembowel his horse. Blade registered the shaggy black and brown coat of fur, the twin snouts and the slavering mouth, the exposed yellow fangs and the four beady eyes, and the two tails and the raking claws in the twinkling before the mutation struck, and then the roan shied to the left, sidestepping into the wall of trees on that side.

Blade saw the mutant rip its right paw along the roan's belly, leaving red streaks in its wake, and he perceived the horse would go down or pin him against a tree before he could bring the Mossberg into effective play. Consequently, without a second thought, he released his shotgun and dove from the saddle, straight at the mutant, his right hand curling around the right Bowie hilt, his left reaching for the beast.

Intent on tearing at the yielding, rich flesh of the horse, the mutant did not bother to look any higher than the roan's shoulder. The first inkling the creature had that something was amiss was when a heavy body crashed into its back and a powerful arm clamped around its throat.

Blade and the mutant tumbled to the ground, rolling and thrashing in the dirt, Blade with a tenuous grip on the enraged beast, the abomination striving to tear the presumptuous human to ribbons. They collided with a tree and reversed direction.

Somewhere, someone shouted the Warrior's name.

Blade sank the gleaming Bowie into the mutation again and again and again, feeling his left forearm sting as claws sliced his skin. The mutant jostled and twisted and pitched, and Blade started to lose his grip. Vision of those claws cutting into his throat inspired him to cling on for dear life, and always the knife went in, in, in.

More yelling arose nearby.

In the recesses of his mind, on an unconscious level of recognition, Blade knew the Kid must be near at hand and recognized the youthful gunman was yelling for him to get out of the way so the Kid could fire. But the beast would turn on Blade the moment he released its throat, so he held on and stabbed. He lost count of the number of times he imbedded the big knife to the hilt, and still the mutant struggled to break free.

A gunshot cracked.

And then Blade rammed into another tree and his left arm went momentarily numb. Instantly the mutant spun and lunged at his neck, and Blade instinctively speared the Bowie into the creature's throat, up and in under the chin. The beast hissed once, then collapsed, blood pouring from its open mouth, its lifeless eyes wide.

"Blade!" Kid Zanto called.

The Warrior shoved the mutation from him, jerking the Bowie out, and rose slowly. Every muscle in his body seemed to ache, and his shoulders and upper arms were oddly stiff. Blood, dirt, and gore caked his clothing.

"You're okay!" the Kid exclaimed.

Blade looked up.

Kid Zanto, Arnie, and Brount were astride their animals, six feet away, the Kid on the right and Arnie in the center. Arnie looked like he wanted to be somewhere else, and understandably so. The Kid held his right Ruger pointed in the general direction of the fedora.

"What happened?" Blade asked.

"I couldn't get a clear shot," the Kid stated angrily, his flinty gaze on Arnie. "None of us could. But this jackass tried to use the Uzi. I came close to parting his hair."

The Warrior inhaled deeply, his gray eyes narrowing as he stared at Arnie. "You tried to use the Uzi? I would have been shot to pieces along with the mutant."

"I wasn't going to use the Uzi," Arnie countered. "The Kid made a mistake."

"I never make a mistake," Kid Zanto declared angrily.

Brount cleared his throat and edged his horse closer to the Warrior. "It was a mistake. I know Arnie wouldn't have tried to bag the mutant with you right there."

"I wonder," Blade said.

"Yeah," Arnie said, and committed a blunder of monumental proportions. He smirked. "You know me."

"Yeah, I know you," Blade mimicked, and threw the Bowie overhand, his massive physique uncoiling like a whip, his right arm streaking up, down, and out in a toss he had practiced innumerable times.

The bloody blade sped the intervening six feet and thudded squarely in the center of Arnie's chest, jolting him, shocking him witless for the space of two seconds. "What the hell!" he blurted out, then glanced at Brount in bewilderment, dropped the Uzi, and pitched to the road.

Transfixed by the sight, stunned by the suddenness of the assault, Brount gaped at the prone form on the ground. When he twisted toward the giant, he saw the left Bowie out and ready to finish the job should Arnie unexpectedly rise.

"Son of a bitch!" the Kid breathed in awe.

Daniel Brount watched Blade move to Arnie and retrieve the other knife, and as he watched, a chill breeze cooled the anger flaring in his cheeks. "What the hell did you do that for?" he snapped, controlling himself with an effort.

"He pushed me one time too many," Blade responded, wiping the right Bowie clean on Arnie's fedora.

"He was my right-hand man, my second in command," Brount complained. "You've already killed Butch, and I was grooming him to fill in for Arnie. Where am I going to find someone to fill their shoes?"

Blade rose, sliding the Bowies into their sheaths, and stared at Brount. "You're looking at him."

"What?" Brount said, and blinked a few times, his mouth working soundlessly. He glanced at Arnie, then at Blade.

To Kid Zanto the happenings of the past few minutes had left him flabbergasted. He'd seen his newfound giant friend take on a mutant and win. He'd seen Arnie die swiftly and efficiently. And now, if he understood correctly, Blade was applying for Arnie's old job. The giant confused him like no other man ever had, and yet he felt drawn to the man in the black leather vest in a bond of abiding friendship. He looked at Brount, expecting his employer to explode, and received another surprise when his boss burst into laughter.

Blade waited, his hands on his hips, suspicious the laughter might be a ruse to throw him off guard so Brount could draw those Heckler and Koch double-action 45's.

"I get it!" Brount declared happily. "I get it!"

What did he get? the Kid wondered, and twirled his Redhawk into its holster.

Brount pointed at Arnie and slapped his thigh, venting more mirth. "First Butch, and now Arnie! You wanted the job for yourself! The whole damn time you wanted the job for yourself!" He cackled and shook his head.

The Warrior remained quiet.

"I knew you were smart, but I didn't realize how smart,"

Brount said, and chuckled. "You had this planned all along."

"If you say so," Blade said noncommittally.

"There's no need to be offended. I admire a man with guts and initiative."

"Do I get the job?"

Brount regarded the Warrior critically. "To tell you the truth, I couldn't ask for a better man. It'll take you a while to learn all the ropes, and there will be grumblings from a few who have worked for me for a long time."

"I'll handle them," Blade promised.

"I bet you will," Brount agreed, and laughed.

"I'll take the job on one condition."

Brount abruptly ceased laughing and his features hardened. "Are you presuming to dictate terms to me?"

"I wouldn't dream of usurping your authority," Blade replied. "My condition is reasonable, and it's probably one you might make yourself."

"Let's hear it."

"I'll accept the job as your second in command if you'll allow me to appoint the Kid as my assistant, my own right-hand man, so to speak."

Kid Zanto's mouth dropped.

"Your condition is reasonable," Brount concurred. "Yeah, I like the idea. You're now my second in command, and the Kid will work under you." He paused and snickered. "Who knows? Between the two of you, you might be able to get the job done." He wheeled his horse and headed for town without a word of remorse for the fallen Arnie.

A psychopath, Blade concluded, and moved to reclaim the Mossberg. He picked up the shotgun and wiped dirt from the barrel, and then realized the Kid was staring at him. "Yes?"

"I don't know what to make of you."

"My wife says the same thing all the time."

"You're married?"

"We'd better catch up with Brount."

The Kid leaned forward. "Why'd you pick me?"

"Maddie can't shoot as straight."

"I'm serious."

Blade went to reply, when he saw Daniel Brount rein in and glance back at them.

"As your first official act, I'd like you two to get your asses in gear! I want to reach Shantytown sometime this year!"

CHAPTER TEN

Blade took to the job readily, determined to impress Brount, and put in long hours the first week, working from dawn until midnight every day. He made daily rounds of all Brount's joints, inspecting the books and attending to sundry minor problems. He supervised the collection squads responsible for collecting the weekly protection fees from all the other businesses in Shantytown. He arranged work schedules for all of Brount's employees. Everywhere he went, Kid Zanto stayed at his side. During work hours the two were inseparable and they became fast friends. At night Blade slept on Maddie's couch, while the Kid invariably slept at the apartment of his sweetheart, the prostitute named Susie.

As Brount had foretold, a handful of his men protested the Warrior's promotion. They claimed they should have been selected by virtue of their seniority. Brount dispensed with all objections and arguments suavely. He told them his decision was final, but they were certainly welcome to voice their protests to Blade, and if any of them felt so inclined, they could exercise their right to challenge the new second in command for his post. No one elected to exercise their right.

Blade attended a rigged auction on the third day of his job, at which a Brount partisan received title to the Neblette farm. He became fully aware of the political ploys, the secret deals and dirty tricks, Brount employed to solidify his control over the territory.

The Warrior also learned a fascinating secret. Although most of Brount's business affairs were duly recorded in thick, heavy ledgers, Brount carried on his person a small black book rumored to contain information pertaining to secret deals and contacts. An old-timer inadvertently tipped the Warrior off one night at a bar, and Blade heard the story confirmed by several of Brount's employees during the course of seemingly idle conversations when he just happened to direct their discussion around to the subject of the rumored black book, a book Blade wanted to get his hands on.

One week after the gunfight at the Neblette farm, as Blade and the Kid relaxed at the bar at the Booze N' Broads, a man burst into the room yelling at the top of his lungs.

"Help! Help! They're wrecking the joint!"

All activity ceased, and Blade and the Kid pushed through the crowd to where the man leaned on a table for support and gasped for air.

The Warrior recognized the man as Jenks, a gambler who plied his trade at an establishment known as the Acey Deucey located two blocks south of the Booze N' Broads.

"Blade!" Jenks exclaimed. "Thank goodness!"

"What's wrong?"

"You've got to get to the Acey Duecey right away. They've already knifed the bouncer, Stoner, and cut up the bartender, Gloria, pretty bad," Jenks detailed.

"Who did, Jenks?" Blade asked calmly.

"There's five of 'em, all wearing animal-hide clothes and smelling like they haven't washed in years. I think they're trappers from the far north. They drank too much and got rowdy, and when Stoner tried to cool them down, the biggest one gutted him with a knife."

"Do they all have guns?"

"Yeah," Jenks nodded. "Rifles. Maybe a few pistols too. I got the hell out of there. Slipped through the side door and came straight here."

"Mister Brount will see that you're properly rewarded for your service," Blade said, remembering the instructions Brount had given him with respect to *always* offering money for services rendered, no matter hows small or insignificant the services might be. He motioned at the Kid and hurried to the door.

"Five to two ain't bad odds," Kid Zanto remarked.

Blade paused just outside the door, the cold night air tingling his skin, and debated his next move. The Acey Deucey was another of Brount's own businesses, not merely another joint that paid protection. Whenever a nasty situation developed at any of Brount's establishments, reinforcements were to be dispatched immediately. Blade knew Brount was at a tavern on the extreme north side of town. "I want you to go find Brount," he said.

"What? Why?"

"He should be informed right away."

"But what about you? You can't take them all on by your lonesome," the Kid objected.

"Don't worry about me. I won't do anything stupid. Go find Brount. Now."

The Kid headed northward. "All right. But I don't like this one bit," he grumbled, and quickly disappeared in the darkness.

Blade sprinted to the south, oblivious to the pedestrians he passed, concentrating on how to deal with the five trappers. He hoped to avoid further bloodshed, and had sent the Kid after Brount so he wouldn't need to keep one eye on the impetuous gunfighter. If the violence escalated, innocent bystanders might be harmed.

A throng had gathered outside the Acey Deucey, the

spectators standing well into the street, away from the door and the windows. From within sounded the breaking of glass and the smashing of wood. A woman wailed pitiably.

The Warrior slowed and drew within ten yards of the front door.

"Here comes Blade!" a man shouted.

"He'll teach those pricks!" added another.

Blade advanced cautiously toward a window positioned near the northwest corner of the building, the Mossberg held firmly in his brawny hands. The wailing abruptly stopped as he stepped to the corner of the narrow window, one of the few in Shantytown actually incorporating a glass pane, and peered inside.

The interior of the Acey Deucey looked like a tornado had struck it. All of the tables and chairs had been overturned or busted into bits. Broken glasses and mugs littered the floor. Lined against the walls on the right and the left were the patrons, perhaps three dozen all told, all with their arms upraised, many showing their fear. Lying in the center of the floor, doubled over on his right side, was the bouncer, Stoner, his intestines forming a pulpy mound next to his body, blood dribbling from his open mouth, his lifeless eyes locked on empty space.

In front of the bar, on her back on the floor, her arms screening her face, lay the barkeep, a woman named Gloria. Her yellow blouse had been torn from her body and tossed onto the counter. Thin red lines, razor-fine knife slits, marred her quivering pale flesh. She began wailing again.

Blade focused on the five men responsible, his temper boiling at the treatment accorded the woman.

The five trappers were a filthy, uncombed, disheveled lot. All five had rifles slung over their shoulders, and three of them wore cartridge belts. They were also armed with ten-inch skinning knives, and one trapper, apparently the leader, a mountain of a man with a stringy black beard, stood over Gloria and taunted her while waving his skinning knife in his left hand and holding a bottle of Scotch in his right.

Blade ducked below the window and edged over to the door, which had been left open a crack. He eased the door inward until he could see the entire room.

The leader had spit a mouthful of Scotch onto Gloria's breasts. Two of his companions were collecting valuables from the patrons, while the third leaned against the bar guzzling whiskey and the fourth covered the customers with a revolver.

Gloria whimpered and squirmed.

The sight of the woman in torment altered the Warrior's perspective. He'd envisioned the trappers as five hard-working men who'd come to town for a fun time and let drink get the better of them. Instead, he found a quintet of hulking degenerates, each on a par with the mutation he'd slain returning from the Neblette farm, each one savage and unpredictable and utterly devoid of compassion.

Gloria howled with dismay when the leader leaned down and roughly squeezed her right breast.

"How's that, you snotty bitch?" the trapper demanded. "So you think you're too good for us, huh? Well, I'll learn you different before I'm done."

"You tell her, Trask!" the trapper covering the customers declared.

Blade has seen more than enough. He slid into the Acey Deucey, his back to the wall, the Mossberg level. "Drop your weapons!" he commanded, anticipating the trappers would be startled by his unexpected appearance and he would be able to disarm them relatively easily.

No such luck.

The five stared at him with supreme disinterest, indicating they were either extremely inebriated or extremely confident in their ability to handle all comers.

"Drop your weapons!" Blade repeated.

They went about their business in an unhurried fashion.

Confounded, Blade took a stride forward. "Didn't you hear me? I told you to drop your weapons!"

"Get lost, moron!" the trapper holding the revolver barked.

"Yeah," chimed in the one guzzling the whiskey. "Get lost before we teach you not to stick your big nose in where it isn't wanted!"

"You don't understand," Blade said. "There are others on their way here right this second. If you don't submit quietly, you'll all be killed."

"Submit, hell!" bellowed Trask. "We haven't hit a big city since last fall, and we aim to celebrate."

Blade nodded at the bartender. "Is that your idea of celebrating?"

"She wouldn't let me feel her titty," Trask replied angrily. "No woman says no to me."

The Warrior's stomach muscles tightened. "This is your last warning. Drop your weapons."

A short, solidly built trapper involved in collecting valuables from the patrons glanced at the Warrior. "Hell! I'm tired of listenin' to this peckerwood." An Astra revolver materialized in his left hand, from out of the folds of his bear coat, and he touched the barrel to the head of his nearest customer and smirked. "Put down that dinky shotgun of yours, mister, or this pilgrim is dog meat."

Blade hesitated, chiding himself for his stupidity. His misplaced impulse to refrain from harming the trappers and avoid having any of the innocent bystanders injured had placed him in a bind.

"I ain't got all day, jerk," the trapper said.

He couldn't possibly cut loose with two of the trappers standing among the customers. Gritting his teeth in frustration, Blade lowered the Mossberg to the floor.

"Now raise your arms over your head," the same trapper directed.

Blade complied, his gray eyes becoming steely.

"Want me to shoot him in the nuts?" asked the trapper covering the customers.

"No, not yet," Trask growled. "We want to have our fun first, don't we?"

The pair who had been gathering the valuables strolled toward the Warrior.

"Ain't he a sizable lug?" commented the trapper armed with the Astra.

"He's as big as Trask," the second one remarked.

"Maybe he'd like to wrestle," Astra said, and snickered.

They halted a yard away and studied the giant.

Blade held his body still, but his mind raced. None of the trappers were near the customers now, so the bystanders wouldn't be in the line of fire if he could get his hands on the Mossberg. But how could he accomplish the feat with the two trappers standing right there in front of him? He wished heartily for a distraction, and to his complete astonishment a distraction came on the scene seconds later in the form of the last person he would have expected to see: Zed.

The apish bodyguard sauntered into the Acey Deucey acting as if he didn't have a care in the world. Black and blue bruises discolored his features, and a white bandage, a wad of cloth applied by the only man in Shantytown who came close to resembling a doctor, covered his crudely reconstructed nostrils. He held his right elbow next to his chest, favoring the side where Blade had broken a rib.

Astra glanced at the newcomer and gawked. "Damn, mister! What the hell happened to you?"

Zed gazed at each of the trappers in turn before answering. "I got the crap beat out of me."

"We can see that," Astra said. "Did you get in a few licks of your own?"

"I hardly touched him," Zed replied solemnly.

"Whew! I can't imagine anyone stompin' someone with all the muscles you've got. Who beat you up?" Astra asked.

Zed grinned and pointed at the Warrior. "He did."

"Really?" Astra said.

Blade's lips compressed into slits and he clenched his

hands. Of all the luck! Had Zed seen him enter the Acey Deucey, or was the bodyguard's arrival a coincidence? He hadn't spoken to Zed since their fight. The doctor had ordered the bodyguard to rest in bed as much as possible.

"Really," Zed confirmed.

The three other trappers approached, their interest aroused by the unique situation. Trask shouldered Astra aside and jabbed his right thumb into the Warrior's sternum.

"So this son of a bitch whomped you, huh?"

"He sure did," Zed stated.

A cruel grin creased Trask's hairy visage. "How would you like a chance to get even?"

"How's that?" Zed queried, sounding puzzled.

"How would you like to stomp this busybody into the floor?"

"When?"

"Here and now, you idiot. We'll make sure nobody butts in, and we'll keep this bastard covered so he doesn't try to use his hands or feet," Trask said.

"You mean I can beat on him to my heart's content?" Zed questioned.

"That's exactly what I mean," Trask declared. "What do you say?"

Zed stared at the Warrior, his mouth curling upwards. "I like the idea."

"Figured you would," Trask said, chuckling.

"One of my ribs is busted, and I can't swing my arm very hard," Zed mentioned.

"Use your boots," Trask suggested.

Zed nodded at a table leg lying on the floor to the right. "How about letting me use that?"

Trask glanced at the stout leg and snickered. "Be my guest, pilgrim."

Slowly, deliberately, Zed stepped to the table leg and leaned down, grunting as his thick fingers closed on the wood. He straightened with an effort and hefted the makeshift club, satisfied with the weight and the feel. "This should do nicely,'' he commented.

''Hit him on the nose first,'' Astra advised.

''No, smack him on the knee. They break like eggshells,'' remarked the trapper holding the whiskey bottle.

''Wallop the stuffin' out of the chump,'' recommended a third.

Zed walked up to the Warrior and looked Blade in the eyes. ''I owe you,'' the bodyguard said, and raised the table leg overhead.

Blade tensed, ready for the worst, knowing Zed and the trappers possessed an insurmountable advantage and prepared to give an accounting of himself they would long remember. Then, to his profound amazement, Zed grinned at him and winked.

''Yeah, I owe you,'' the bodyguard reiterated, ''for sparing my life.'' And with that pronouncement he whirled and brought the table leg crashing down upon Trask's skull.

Blade had no opportunity to observe the result. He was already in motion, delivering a kick to the genitals of the trapper armed with the Astra, dropping the man on the spot. He pivoted, his right fist swinging in an arc, and clipped the other trapper who had a revolver out on the chin, sending the man stumbling backwards to trip over his own feet and sprawl onto the floor.

Zed and Trask were grappling, on their knees.

The trapper holding the whiskey bottle clawed at a skinning knife in a sheath on his left hip, while the fifth trapper tried to unlimber a Marlin rifle slung over his left shoulder.

Blade crouched and scooped up the Mossberg in a smooth motion, and he pumped the shotgun twice in swift succession. With each thundering shot one of the trappers was flung to the floor, torn nearly in half by the buckshot.

Astra had scrambled to his hands and knees, his features bright red, and aimed the revolver at the Warrior.

With a deft twist Blade threw himself to the left and fired, the Mossberg bucking in his hands.

The heavy slugs took Astra full in the face, blowing his

nose and part of his eyes outward in a shower of crimson and pulp, and he flipped onto his back and was still.

Blade worked the slide action again, the blast hitting the trapper he'd slugged as the man rose to his knees. The impact bowled the man over.

Leaving only Zed and Trask, who were wrestling on the floor, rolling back and forth, straining and heaving. Zed, in his weakened state, barely held his own.

Rising quickly, the Warrior moved toward them, watching for an opening, which came five seconds later when Trask pinned Zed and the trapper raised his head to roar in impending triumph. No sooner had the cry died when Blade pressed the Mossberg barrel to the right side of Trask's hairy head and squeezed the trigger.

Zed recoiled as particles of flesh, bone, and hair rained down on his face and neck, and he grimaced as blood splattered on his skin. He looked upward, aghast at beholding a headless corpse straddling his torso, and in revulsion he bucked and shoved and sent the trapper's body sailing through the air to smack against the far wall.

The onlookers had seemingly grown roots.

Frowning in disgust, Zed wiped at the moist chunks and pieces clinging to his skin. He glanced upward when a hand extended into his line of vision.

"Need a lift?"

"Thanks," Zed said, taking the Warrior's proffered hand and using the added leverage to stand.

"I should be the one thanking you," Blade responded. "You bailed me out of a fix."

"Then we're even. I know Brount wanted you to kill me, and I know you wouldn't. I don't quite know what to make of you, Blade, but you're all right in my book," Zed stated with conviction.

The Warrior surveyed the carnage grimly. "How about if I have someone clean this mess, and I'll treat you to a drink?"

Zed grinned. "Fine by me, if you'll let me return the

favor.''

''Do you know where we can buy some milk?''

''Milk?'' Zed repeated in astonishment, and laughed. ''And folks say *I'm* addle-brained.''

CHAPTER ELEVEN

Two days later Blade and Kid Zanto were walking north on Main Street when Zed approached at a run.

"Blade! Blade!"

"Looks like the gorilla has taken a shine to you," the Kid joked, squinting in the bright morning sunlight.

"Zed is a human being and he deserves the same respect you do," Blade said. "He's also my friend."

"And I know what that means," the Kid cracked.

"We're all children of the Spirit," the Warrior declared enigmatically.

Before the Kid could ask for an explanation, Zed reached them.

"Blade! Mister Brount sent me to fetch you," Zed declared. "He wants you to come to the Booze N' Broads right away."

"Then let's go," Blade said, and together they continued to the north, having five blocks to cover to reach the Booze N' Broads.

"What's all the excitement about?" the Kid inquired.

"A wagon train," Zed disclosed. "Camped two miles

from town."

"Haven't seen one of those in eight, maybe nine months," the Kid commented.

"Does this wagon train carry trading supplies?" Blade asked.

Kid Zanto snorted. "You don't understand. Wagon trains pass through the territory fairly frequently during the warm months. If they're big and the people are well armed, we leave them alone. But if they're small and they don't have many guns, we raid them."

"You raid unprotected wagon trains?" Blade queried, his tone laced with accusation.

"Hey, I didn't start the practice," the Kid responded. "The Union was raidin' wagon trains before I was born."

"And everyone knows about the raids?"

"Most folks."

"Why don't the people put a stop to it?"

"Get real. Who's going to stand up against the Union? They wouldn't last two seconds."

Blade digested the information, scowling and hefting the Mossberg. Every time he ventured beyond the walled ramparts of the Home, he grew more thankful to the Founder, the survivalist who had constructed the compound in northwestern Minnesota prior to World War Three. If not for Kurt Carpenter's foresight in building the retreat and in stocking the 30-acre refuge with enormous quantities of essential, durable provisions, the Family would not exist. The brutal, despicable conditions in the Outlands and elsewhere would have eradicated Carpenter's descendants decades ago. The Founder had forecast the decline of civilization after the nuclear holocaust and taken wise precautions to ensure his followers persisted in a world gone mad. Twenty-foot-high brick walls, barbed wire, and a moat were only the initial defenses. A gigantic armory containing a host of versatile weaponry provided the firepower the Family needed to presevere amid all the mutants, scavangers, and raiders.

The mere thought of what would happen if those brick

walls should ever be breached successfully brought goose bumps to Blade's flesh. So far, for 106 years, the Family had withstood all assaults. So far. He abruptly became aware of Zed speaking.

"—has seven men all set to go as soon as we reach the Booze N' Broads. I can't go 'cause of my rib."

"Who found the train?" the Kid asked.

"Dolon. He was taking a shortcut back from his sweetheart's, that farm girl Beth who lives out east, when he spotted smoke and snuck close for a look. You know Beth and him are getting married."

The Kid snickered.

"Don't you intend to marry some day?" Blade snapped.

"Yeah, sure, but—" Kid Zanto started to reply.

"Then who are you to make fun of Dolon?" Blade queried testily, and increased his speed to walk by himself.

Thoroughly confused, the Kid looked at Zed. "What did I do?"

Zed simply shrugged.

They covered the remaining distance in silence, with the Warrior brooding, the Kid sulking, and Zed wondering what the hell was going on.

Blade spied the ten mounts saddled and waiting outside the tavern. Lounging near the building were seven of Brount's hired guns, among them the 20-year-old with blond hair and blue eyes named Dolon.

Daniel Brount emerged and gazed down Main Street, smiling when he caught sight of the giant and the gunfighter. "Blade! Are you in for a treat!"

"So I've heard," the Warrior replied.

"Dolon spotted a wagon train with four wagons, and all four are filled with personal effects. We're riding out now," Brount said, and pointed at a black stallion. "I've obtained a horse for you that isn't skittish."

"Thanks."

"Mount up, boys, and let's ride!" Brount bellowed.

In short order the ten men were riding south along Main

Street until they came to the second intersection. Brount led them to the east, sticking to the secondary street as far as it went, then heading overland toward a ridge perhaps a mile off.

Blade rode near the head of the column, between Brount and the Kid, immersed in reflection. In five more days Brount was due to head for the conference with Crusher Payne, and Brount had still not revealed whether the Warrior would be going along. Blade didn't want to press the issue for fear of being too obvious, of appearing too eager. He'd hoped he would automatically be privileged to attend as Brount's second in command, but when he'd idly broached the topic of the conference to the Kid, Zanto had mentioned that sometimes Arnie had gone and sometimes Arnie had stayed in Shantytown. Blade needed to be at that conference. He was impatient to trace the weapons to their source and return to the Home, and he suspected Crusher of being that source.

"I don't know why these fools bother crossing the Outlands in wagons," Brount mentioned conversationally. "Three-fourths of them don't live to complete the journey. Most of them are probably seeking a better life elsewhere." He laughed. "There is no better life."

"Where do they come from?" Blade questioned.

"Points east, mostly," Brount answered. "Whenever a large train stops at Shantytown, we throw out the red carpet and overcharge the bastards like crazy. I always turn a tidy profit on wagon trains."

"They must need to buy a lot of supplies," Blade noted slyly, seizing the occasion to extract crucial intelligence.

"You don't know the half of it," Brount said, shaking his head. "Those fools will buy everything that isn't bolted down. Food, clothes, feed, you name it."

"Weapons?" Blade commented casually.

"I do a brisk business in weapons," Brount confided. "Machine guns and semiautomatics are hot items, although few can afford them. Revolvers and rifles are the mainstay of my arms business."

"You must receive your shipments from Crusher," Blade said while gazing at the ridge, afraid Brount might detect the expectation in his features.

"Yeah," Brount verified. "Crusher has access to an unlimited supply of weapons, and some of the guns were manufactured in the last five years or so."

"Recently manufactured? How's he manage that feat?"

"Certain matters are kept secret," Brount responded sternly.

"Sorry. I wasn't prying."

"I know. But I've told you all I can. If Crusher likes you, maybe he'll fill you in himself."

Blade could scarcely restrain the excitement within him, and he coughed before speaking. "I'll get to meet him?"

"Sure. Didn't I tell you? In five days there's a meeting taking place down near Trego."

"I knew about the meeting, but I didn't know if I'd be tagging along."

"You will," Brount said. "I want Crusher to meet my new second in command. I think the two of you will hit it off."

"I hope so."

In ten minutes they came to the base of the sloping ridge. A narrow trail wound to the top, and Brount followed the trail expertly, managing his horse with consummate ease, a skillful, polished rider.

As Blade watched Brount ascend the ridge, he wondered if his newfound employer was equally adept at handling the double-action 45's. He'd never observed Brount using the pistols, but he doubted the man wore them simply for show.

They crested the ridge onto a plain stretching to the north and the south, and on the rim a bitter wind swept into them. Hunched against the cold, they rode to the east, and in less than a mile they came to a ravine on their right. Brount waved them into the ravine, where they dismounted and gathered around.

"You lead us from here," Brount directed Dolon.

The blond hired gun, who packed two Colts and a Winchester, moved off down the ravine, proceeding slowly, stealthily.

Blade found himself walking third in line, behind Brount, and he racked his brain for a solution to his quandary. Blameless travelers were about to be butchered, and if he interfered he would lose all hope of avenging the slain Moles. If he did nothing, he would have innocent lives on his conscience. What should he do? he asked himself. What *could* he do?

Forty yards later Dolon halted behind a towering boulder. The ravine ran straight for ten yards, then angled sharply to the right. "Take a peek," Dolon whispered to Brount.

"Come with me," Brount said softly to the Warrior.

Together they skirted the boulder and crept to the bend in the ravine. Brount flattened his back against the earth wall and risked a fleeting glance around the corner. He drew back, smiled, and nodded at Blade.

Dreading what he would see, Blade knelt and peered past the edge. Eight yards beyond, the ravine ended in a natural bowl or depression. Part of the south side of the bowl had collapsed long ago, leaving a gradual incline, a ramp, from the top to the bottom. Four wagons were parked near the ramp, the horses tied close at hand. A roaring fire blazed in the middle of the bowl, sending gray and black smoke swirling skyward, and gathered about the fire, warming themselves, talking and joking, were eight men.

Blade felt a sensation of relief. At least there weren't any women and children! He noticed all of the men were armed. The wagons were flatbeds, heaped high with articles or boxes, but the cargo was covered by sturdy canvas and concealed from view. He felt a tap on the arm and glanced up.

Brount jerked his thumb toward the others.

The Warrior trailed Brount to the enormous boulder and crouched next to him as the paid killers huddled to receive their instructions.

"I don't believe it!" Brount hissed.

"What, boss?" one of the men asked.

Brount glanced at Dolon. "You didn't find any ordinary wagon train of pilgrims searching for the good life."

"I didn't?" Dolon responded.

"No," Brount said. "You found Harland Warner."

"Who's he?" Kid Zanto inquired.

"Warner is a miserable black marketeer who operates all around the Great Lakes. He's been a thorn in the organization's side for twenty-five years. The son of a bitch refuses to pay us our fair percentage of his take in our territories. He claims he doesn't do business in our region, but we've known he does. Until now, we've never been able to catch him in the act," Brount said and rubbed his hands together in anticipation. "Well, I've caught him! Crusher will be extremely pleased if I can wipe Warner out. He sent a man to Warner about ten years ago, demanding that Warner pay up. Warner sent the messenger's head back in a plastic bag."

Blade lowered his eyes to the ground so no one would observe his grin. What a relief! Harland Warner and his cronies could hardly be considered innocent travelers. If Warner was a black-market kingpin, then he undoubtedly dabbled in more than illicit trade. Blade could participate in the raid without reservations.

"Listen up!" Brount said. "I don't want Warner to slip through our fingers. Kid, take three men and work your way around to the south side, to the top of the ramp. Take out any lookouts and wait for us to start shooting. That'll be your signal to come down the ramp." He paused and surveyed his men. "We don't take prisoners. Understood?"

The hired guns nodded.

"Then let's get cracking," Brount prompted them.

The Kid picked three men and retraced their route for 15 yards before angling up the south wall of the ravine. The steep incline, composed of lose soil, afforded slippery footing, and they climbed slowly until near the rim. At that point they flattened and crawled from sight.

Brount crouched. "I spotted Warner near the fire they have going," he told his men. "He's wearing a black hat and a brown coat and carrying an M-16. He has gray hair and a gray mustache. Whoever nails him receives a bonus of ten gold coins."

A sparkle lit the eyes of the killers.

"Let's do it," Brount said, and rose. He drew his pistols and headed for the bend.

The Mossberg firmly in his hands, Blade stayed next to Brount. They stopped shy of the bend and Brount eased to the edge for a look. Blade squatted and moved forward, peering once again at the encampment.

A ninth man was now visible on the skyline, pacing back and forth near the ramp, a rifle in his hands, keeping guard. The eight around the fire were still oblivious to the danger closing in on them, still chatting and laughing.

Blade suspected Warner and his men were holed up for the day. He reasoned the black marketeers would likely travel at night in the territories controlled by the Union. Building a fire seemed careless, but Warner might not expect trouble so far off the beaten path. Possibly Warner had used this same spot on many occasions and felt safe.

Brount motioned at his men, directing them to fan across the ravine, which they immediately did, their bodies low among the rocks.

A tense minute elapsed.

Blade leaned against the wall, thinking of his wife and son, hoping he wouldn't be slain in a meaningless squabble between vultures like Brount and Warner, and wondering if the Kid's party would be able to dispose of the lookout without difficulty.

Apparently they couldn't.

Because a moment later rifle fire erupted from the bowl rim.

CHAPTER TWELVE

The gunfire turned out to be advantageous.

Brount waved his right arm and charged around the bend, drawing the 45's, and on his heels came his men.

Harland Warner's men were taken completely unawares. They had swung toward the ramp at the sound of the shots, mistakenly assuming the source of the attack came from that direction, and consequently had their backs to the ravine. Three of them were down before they awoke to their mistake.

Blade intentionally brought up the rear, having scant relish for the battle at hand, intent on merely staying alive. He saw Brount's killers blast away, and saw a trio of black marketeers die violently, and then Warner's men were returning the fire, with five of them employing automatic or semiautomatic arms. They were quite skilled, making every shot count and slaying two of Brount's hired guns with their initial volley. Blade dove for cover in the shelter of a waist-high boulder and listened to the deafening booming and crackling.

Nearby a man screamed in torment.

The firing reached a crescendo, then tapered as the

participants on both sides sought protection behind the handiest sanctuary.

The sound of pounding boots reached Blade's ears, and he raised up on his elbows and peered toward the bowl. Several corpses dotted the ground, and he glimpsed others who had taken refuge, but his attention fixed on the two men who were racing directly at him. Astounded, he had only seconds to react, and his mind seemed sluggish in responding, unable to credit the evidence of his eyes.

Harland Warner and one other were coming straight toward him!

In a twinkling the Warrior perceived that Warner must believe the enemy had him trapped. So rather than flee up the ramp and expose himself to enemy bullets, Warner had opted to carry the fight to his foes and escape out the only other available avenue, namely the ravine.

Warner and his henchman were firing wildly at the rocks and boulders, striving to keep Brount and company pinned down, and so far they were succeeding.

Blade knew they would see him. He had nowhere to hide, nowhere to run, and the circumstances dictated his next move. Whipping the Mossberg to his shoulder, he pumped the shotgun twice at a range of less than eight feet.

Harland Warner and his companion appeared to slam into an invisible wall. Their bodies halted abruptly and they were hurled backwards, all in the blink of an eye, both with their chests ruptured.

The Warrior dropped behind the boulder again, expecting to become the target of Warner's men, but not a single shot zinged in his direction. Instead there were a few desultory rounds, then a brief silence. Finally a gruff voice called out.

"Whoever the hell you are, we give up!"

"Then throw out your weapons where we can see them and stand with your hands in the air!" commanded Brount.

Blade heard the clatter of automatic rifles and other guns striking the earth.

"None of you move!" barked Brount.

Cautiously, poking the Mossberg out first, Blade straightened, surveying the ravine and the bowl, taking a tally. The lookout lay on his back on the ramp, dead. Kid Zanto and the three with him were descending the ramp on the double. Three of Warner's crew had survived the gunfight, although one stood unsteadily, a bright red stain marking his left shoulder. Only three of Brount's men had been killed, all told, and the rest converged warily on their prisoners.

Brount walked toward the Warrior, smiling and gesturing animatedly with the pistols. "We did it! We nailed the son of a bitch!" He stopped and stared at his slain nemesis. "I should say *you* did it. I saw you bag them." He looked up. "Hiring you on was the smartest move I've made. You've more than earned the ten gold coins."

"Just doing my job," Blade said, with what he hoped qualified as the appropriate humility.

"Wait until I tell Crusher about this!" Brount said, elated, and walked toward the prisoners.

Blade came forward, gazing at Harland Warner's contorted features, then the henchman's, and at one of Brount's men lying in a disjointed heap, a hole in the center of his forehead, his blue eyes wide, his blond hair disheveled. The farm girl named Beth would need to find another husband.

"What do you want us to do with these guys?" asked one of the killers guarding Warner's men.

"No prisoners, remember?" Brount said, and shot the three men in the head, his hands sweeping up and the pistols belching a shot at each man. The unexpected, brutal suddenness of the deed made Brount's hired guns jump.

Blade saw the brains and bits of skull fly in every direction, and he recoiled in disgust, then recovered his composure before Brount could notice. Mercy, he concluded, was a term alien to Daniel Brount's vocabulary.

The Kid and his three companions joined them.

"These turkeys weren't very tough," the youthful gunman commented blithely, his Redhawks in his hands.

"Tough enough," Brount said stiffly. "What the hell happened on the rim?"

"How do you mean?" the Kid rejoined.

"Do I look like a simpleton?" Brount snapped. "I heard the lookout begin shooting before I was ready."

"I took care of the lookout," the Kid said.

"But not in time. Why did he begin shooting?"

Kid Zanto pursed his lips and coughed lightly. "One of us slipped on a rock and the lookout spotted us."

Brount raked the three other killers with an imperious glare. "And which one of you was so sloppy?"

None of them answered.

"Funny. My ears must not be working. I could have sworn I asked a question," Brount stated sarcastically.

"I did," mumbled a man in jeans and a brown shirt. He carried a Browning.

"You, Henry?"

"Yes, sir," Henry admitted.

"I'm very disappointed in you."

"I know sir," Henry said. "I'm disappointed in myself. It won't happen again, I assure you."

"Damn straight," Brount declared. He smiled condescendingly, and simply fired both semiautomatics from the hip, squeezing off the shots without seeming to consciously aim, a slug tearing through each of hapless Henry's eyes and bursting out the rear of his cranium.

The rest of the killers were dumbfounded.

"You weren't competent enough for me to tolerate your mistakes," Brount said, and spun the pistols into their holsters.

Blade gazed at Henry for a moment, then at his employer. There existed no doubt in his mind now. Brount's expertise extended to handguns as well.

"I want all of Harland's boys searched, and everything you find placed in a saddlebag. Collect all of their weapons," Brount instructed. He nodded at Blade and the Kid. "You two come with me.'' He hurried in the direction of the four wagons.

The Warrior started to comply. He saw the Kid staring at Henry, undisguised loathing etching the youth's countenance. ''Let's go, Kid,'' Blade said softly.

''He had no call to shoot Henry,'' the Kid muttered.

''Don't let him hear you say that,'' Blade advised. ''Come on.''

Kid Zanto nodded once, grimly, and they hastened after Brount, overtaking him in 15 yards.

''I wonder what old Harland was transporting,'' Brount speculated, grinning in excitement.

''Will you turn all four wagons over to Crusher Payne?'' Blade inquired absently.

''I don't have any choice. If I try to divert any merchandise, I'll suffer the same fate as the joker I replaced.''

''Who would know?'' Blade asked, testing Brount's loyalty to Payne.

''Don't even joke about skimming or cheating Crusher,'' Brount warned. ''He has spies everywhere, even in my territory, and he knows everything that goes on. I'd sign my death warrant if I tried to buck him, and I don't want to die the way Mac Volan did.''

''How'd he die?'' Blade queried.

''Crusher had Mac chained to two of the Monster Machines. He gave the signal, and the Monster Machines tore Mac in half,'' Brount detailed, and frowned at the unpleasant memory.

''What are these Monster Machines I've heard so much about?'' the Warrior probed.

''They must be seen to be believed,'' Brount replied. ''One is taller than a full-grown tree and has metal jaws. Another one has a gigantic blade. And the third machine is a humongous truck outfitted with a huge scoop. You'll see them when we travel to the conference.''

"I've been told Crusher possesses other vehicles."

"He does. Cars and trucks."

"Why does he have all the vehicles? Aren't you entitled to have any?"

"There's a reason, but I can't reveal it. Crusher will have to confide in you."

Blade let the subject drop.

They reached the four parked wagons, each piled high with items, the beds obscured by the heavy canvas.

"Unfasten the canvas," Brount commanded.

Blade and the Kid untied the rope securing the canvas to the nearest wagon and slid the canvas aside, revealing stacks of wooden crates in excellent condition.

"What the hell!" Brount blurted. "Blade, open one for me."

The Warrior clambered into the flatbed and inspected the top of the crates. Each had been nailed tight. "They're sealed shut. I'll need a tool to pry the lid."

"Hold on," Kid Zanto said, and went to each of the wagons, checking under the seat. On the third flatbed he found a short iron bar. "I figured they'd have some way of opening the crates," he mentioned, and gave the bar to Blade.

In less than a minute the Warrior forced the top off the uppermost crate closest to the tail of the wagon, then clasped the crate in his massive arms and lowered it to the ground.

Brount squatted and rummaged in the packing material, a peculiar flush to his cheeks, his brow creased. "Ahhhh," he declared, and removed an automatic rifle from the crate, a clean rifle without any nicks or scratches, a rifle that clearly had never been fired. "Damn!"

"A smart piece of hardware," the Kid remarked. "Doesn't look like it's been used."

"It hasn't," Brount snapped, his face contorted in fury. "It's brand new."

"What's wrong, Danny?" the Kid asked. "What's the big deal over a new gun?"

Brount glared at the automatic rifle, not bothering to answer.

Standing in the flatbed with the wind brushing his hair, Blade felt equally elated and mystified. Elated because the rifle Brount held matched one of those confiscated from the raiders, which meant the Warrior was definitely on the right track. And mystified because he couldn't identify the weapon, in itself a singular occurrence. Thanks to the Founder's sagacity in constructing an enormous armory at the Home, the Family possessed sufficient arms to meet the needs of an army. The Warriors, as part of their training, were required to familiarize themselves with every weapon. In addition, scores of books in the Family Library dealt with survival skills, war, and humankind's weaponry down through the ages, and Blade had read every book at least once. Nowhere in the armory, nowhere in any of those books, and nowhere in all his travels had he ever encountered an automatic rifle exactly like the one in Brount's hands. Except once.

When the messenger sent by the Moles had arrived at the Home bearing the tragic news, Blade had departed immediately. He would never forget the grisly sight of all those bloated, ruptured bodies, the men, women, and children butchered without a hope of defending themselves. The leader of the Moles, the arrogant Wolfe, had shown Blade four weapons taken from the raiders slain by the Mole security force after Wolfe had dispatched a 20-man unit in pursuit of the attackers. Not one of the weapons had been alike, and yet all four had appeared to be recently manufactured.

And now here was an automatic rifle that matched perfectly a rifle recovered by the Moles, which confirmed the information supplied by the raider the Moles had captured and tortured. Blade glanced at the crates next to his legs, then at the other wagons. There must be several hundred such weapons in the four wagons, he calculated. Whoever was responsible for manufacturing the new weapons was producing them on a grand scale.

Brount placed the weapon back in the crate and rose. "When Crusher sees this, he'll go berserk." He glanced up at the Warrior. "I want a man to drive each wagon back to Shantytown. We'll tie the unused horses to the rear of the flatbeds."

Blade looked at Kid Zanto. "You heard the man. Pick three men who can handle a wagon. I'll drive this one myself. And send someone up the ravine for our horses."

"On my way," the Kid said, and wheeled and walked off.

In a fit of anger, Brount unexpectedly kicked the crate. "Damn their rotten, conniving souls! The bastards will pay for deceiving us."

Blade jumped to the ground. "I'll put the crate on the wagon," he offered.

"Be sure and cover the crates with the canvas," Brount directed. "I don't want anyone in Shantytown to learn about our cargo. Tell the men I'll cut the tongue out of anyone who blabs."

"Will do."

"It looks like you'll be meeting Crusher sooner than I thought," Brount commented, staring at the rim.

"I will?"

"Yeah. We're leaving for the gravel pit in the morning."

CHAPTER THIRTEEN

The column stretched far along the dusty road en route to the Union headquarters. Blade rode at the head with Brount and Kid Zanto. He twisted in his saddle and looked back at the line, scowling. Six hired guns came next, then the supply wagon and the four flatbeds, while at the rear trailed another six killers. And riding on both sides of each wagon as added protection was yet another thug. Blade fixed his gaze on the supply wagon, on the driver, Zed, and Zed's passenger, and sighed.

Daniel Brount glanced at his second in command and smirked. "Something eating you?"

"Do you always bring a woman along?"

"Never before," Brount admitted.

"Then why bring her?"

"Look, I know the two of you are . . . friends," Brount said, emphasizing the last word. "I can appreciate your concern for her safety, but your moping is starting to bug me. No one will attack us on the way to Trego. No one in their right mind would go up against this many guns."

"But . . ." Blade began, and stopped when Brount held aloft his right arm.

"I haven't finished yet. Wild animals won't come near us, and we can blow away any mutant that gets too close. Maddie is not in any danger, so stop looking at her and sighing. Your damn sighing is driving me nuts."

"Why *did* you bring her, Danny?" the Kid inquired.

"Hell, you too?" Brount responded, and then *he* sighed. "I brought Maddie along because I like to eat."

"What?" came from the Warrior and the gunfighter simultaneously.

"That's right. The trip to headquarters takes two days, so we have to camp out tonight, and I do not intend to eat cold jerky or lumpy canned garbage for my supper," Brount said.

"You brought Maddie along to cook for you?" Blade asked in amazement.

"What else? Finley usually cooks for me on these headquarters trips, but Finley is in Shantytown at this very moment puking his guts out. The man is as sick as a dog. I needed someone to cook, and I offered Maddie a bonus if she would come along. She accepted. It's as simple as that," Brount said testily.

Was it? Blade wondered, doubtful Brount spoke the truth. He recalled the story Maddie had related at her cabin, and he entertained a cynical suspicion there might be an underlying motive to her presence. Brount might have been content to keep his distance after Vern was killed, hoping Maddie would eventually warm to him. But Blade's friendship with her might have aroused Brount to action. Did warped jealousy enter into the picture?

"We'll camp at the spot we normally do," Brount commented. "Five miles from here is a glade and a spring."

They rode in silence for five minutes. Blade listened to the clopping of the hooves and adjusted the Mossberg strap slung over his left shoulder.

"What do you plan to do with the ten gold coins?" Brount asked idly.

Blade patted the brown leather pouch attached to his belt a hand's width from his right Bowie. "I don't know. Thanks again for the pouch."

"I never used it," Brount said, then studied the giant for several seconds. "You know, you're my second in command and I still know very little about you, about your past."

"There's not much to tell."

"For some reason I doubt that. A man doesn't acquire your particular talents by accident. If I'm any judge of men, you've seen a lot of action."

"A bit," Blade acknowledged, puzzled as to why Brount displayed such a sudden interest in his past.

"Ever been to the Twin Cities?"

"Nope," Blade lied.

"A few years ago a pilgrim came through Shantytown who claimed to be from the Twin Cities. Told us a story about a big guy and some friends who took on a gang there and really kicked ass. Wouldn't happen to have been you, would it?"

"No."

"If you don't want to come clean, that's your business," Brount mentioned. "But I should warn you. Crusher has a tremendous curiosity about people. He might not respect your privacy like I do."

"I'll cross that bridge when I come to it."

"Just don't antagonize Crusher. I'd hate to lose such a competent assistant so soon after hiring you."

The afternoon sun climbed high into the sky and sank toward the western horizon. They came to the glade and circled the wagons, and three of the men tended the horses. Four guards were posted and shifts set up for their relief. Zed attended to the fire, while Maddie lowered the supply wagon tailgate and commenced preparing the meal. As she fished a pot and a large spoon out of a wooden box, she spotted Blade walking past the wagon. "Hey! Aren't you speaking to me?"

He halted, then came over. "Of course I am."

"Are you still mad at me because I came?"

"Of course I am," Blade said, and smiled.

"I'll receive a bonus," Maddie mentioned.

"So Brount told me."

"Why are you so annoyed at me?"

"Because I have enough to do without having to worry about you," Blade responded, rankled by her imprudence.

"I won't be a burden," Maddie promised.

"Let's hope not," Blade said, and walked off. He knew he was being excessively hard on her, but her presence put an extra burden on his shoulders. He couldn't dare make a move against Brount or Crusher until he insured Maddie would be safe. Did Brount suspect? he wondered. Was Maddie along as a form of insurance? He spied Zed heading to the west, bearing a bucket, and angled to intercept him. "Where are you going?"

"Getting water for supper."

"I'll tag along," Blade proposed.

They crossed the clearing, making for a stand of brush.

"How's the rib?" Blade inquired.

"Coming along," Zed replied.

"Why didn't you stay in Shantytown and rest?"

Zed shrugged. "I got tired of doing nothing. I wanted to get outdoors."

"At least you get to ride on the wagon with Maddie. The trip shouldn't be boring for you."

"No, it won't be," Zed agreed, and glanced at the Warrior. "She's worried about you, you know."

"Maddie?"

"No, the Tooth Fairy."

Blade gazed at the ground. "What makes you say that?"

"She told me so. Said she came along for two reasons. One was the bonus, the other was to watch over you. She seems to think you're in for a heap of trouble."

"Why?"

"Ask her."

Blade took several strides before speaking again. "Do you like Maddie?"

"What kind of dumb-ass question is that? Sure I like her. We're good buddies," Zed said, and snorted.

"Do you like Brount?"

Zed halted abruptly and faced the Warrior. "What's going on?"

"Nothing. I just asked you a question."

"You're up to something," Zed stated. "I don't know what it is, but you are." He scanned their immediate vicinity, insuring no one could overhear them. "Brount wanted you to kill me, even after you told him you wouldn't, so I figure I don't owe Mister Daniel Brount any damn loyalty. I'll work for him for a while yet, and when the time is ripe I'll pull up stakes."

Blade nodded. "Fair enough. I know we're even, but I have an important request to make."

"What is it?"

"Would you make a point of staying close to Maddie and watching over her without her being aware of you?"

Zed's expression became uncharacteristically thoughtful. "Is Maddie in danger?"

"Could be," Blade responded noncommitally.

"From Brount?"

"Could be."

The bodyguard glanced back at Maddie, busily preparing the meal, and frowned. "There have been rumors floating around for a long time."

"I'd hate for anything to happen to her."

"You and me both," Zed concurred, and looked at Blade. "Okay. I'll watch out for her. If there's any funny business, I'll let you know."

"One more request," the Warrior said.

"Figures."

"If anything should happen to me while we're at the Union headquarters, promise me you'll take Maddie away as quickly as possible?"

"Where would I take her?"

"Head due southwest until you reach the Plains, until you find the Civilized Zone," Blade instructed him.

"I never heard of the place."

"Long ago, during World War Three, the United States government evacuated millions of citizens into the central section of the country. A dictator later took over and the region became known as the Civilized Zone. It's one of seven factions comprising the Freedom Federation."

"The what?"

"The Federation is composed of seven members who have signed a mutual defense treaty, and who are devoted to preserving civilization," Blade elaborated.

Zed scratched his head. "How come you know so much about this stuff?"

"I know."

"What will happen if Maddie and I find the Civilized Zone?" Zed inquired skeptically.

"You'll be welcomed with open arms and given the chance to make new lives for yourselves," Blade assured him.

"They don't kill strangers?"

"No. Every Federation faction exalts the ideal of safe-guarding life, not taking it."

"You sure can use fancy words," Zed remarked, grinning. "All right. I'll do like you say. At the first hint of trouble, I'll take Maddie out of here."

"Thanks, Zed," Blade said, and walked in the direction of the horses, hoping Zed would be as good as his word. He felt relief at having one worry removed, and he was glad he could rely upon Zed as an ally. Engrossed in contemplation, he strolled to the far side of the clearing where the horses were tethered.

A hired gun who liked to wear a buckskin shirt and green pants, a Smith and Wesson on each hip, looked up from brushing a sorrel. "Blade. What's up?"

"Karl, isn't it?"

"That's me," the man said.

"I'm just double-checking. Have all the horses been fed and watered?"

"Every one."

"I've given orders for one guard to stay near the horses at all times," the Warrior said, surveying the forest bordering the clearing on three sides. On the fourth, to the east, lay the road. "I don't like having the trees so close. A horse is a tempting target for any hungry animal or mutation."

"Mister Brount doesn't believe the wildlife will bother us," Karl said. "He's been this way dozens of times."

"Maybe so," Blade stated. "But you know the saying. I'd rather be safe than sorry. If a—" He froze as a blood-curdling shriek arose from the west, from the stand of brush and brown grass surrounding the spring.

"What the hell!" Karl exclaimed.

Blade spun and raced toward the sound, unslinging the shotgun as he ran, a sensation of dread ungulfing him. Others were hurrying across the clearing. The thick vegetation in which the spring was situated, although not as green and lush as it would be during the spring and summer months, effectively shrouded the spring from view. A passerby unaware of the spring's exact location could pass within 15 feet of it and not know it was there. Blade's keen gray eyes probed the shoulder-high brush and low pine trees for a hint of movement.

Kid Zanto approached at an angle on the right, his Rugers out. "What happened?" he called.

The Warrior went to respond, then halted in midstride, gaping as the bushes and trees shook and shivered, and a squat reptilian bulk lumbered into the open, its jaws clamped on Zed's abdomen.

Someone—it must have been Maddie—screamed.

Blade took in the creature's features in a glance. Over six feet in height, the mutation was easily just as wide. A green, moist skin glistened in the fading sunlight. Over seven feet in length, and endowed with bulbous eyes, flaring nostrils, and short, stubby teeth, the mutant incorporated a bizarre mixture of frog, salamander, and alligator traits. Was it a reptile or an amphibian? Had its growth hormones been effected by radioactive or chemical toxins? Why was the thing abroad in such chilly weather? Had the creature staked out the spring as its home, and had Zed appeared to be a tempting morsel? So many imponderables flitted through Blade's mind in the few seconds he stood riveted to the ground. And then he bellowed inarticulately and charged, intending to provoke the monster into dropping Zed and affording a clear line of fire.

The Kid ran forward too, shouting insults.

But instead of releasing Zed or attacking, the mutant began to turn, shuffling slowly, its ponderous legs sluggish, evidently of a mind to return to the spring with its catch.

"No!" Blade cried, and poured on the speed. Zed might still be alive! If the creature sank beneath the water, Zed would be doomed.

The Kid fired two shots into the air, hoping to draw the beast's attention. His shots had the opposite effect. The creature grunted and moved faster.

Damn! Blade fumed. He couldn't shoot at the mutant because he might accidentally hit Zed, yet he also couldn't allow the thing to retreat into the brush. He was ten feet from the beast when it completed its turn, and there, wriggling in the grass like a gigantic worm and luring the Warrior like a fish to bait, twitched and writhed the creature's three-foot tail. Blade tossed the Mossberg aside, taking two leaping strides in the process, and launched himself into the air with his hands outstretched.

Maddie screamed again.

The Warrior came down hard on his stomach and knees, his hands clutching at the slippery tail and securing a firm hold. He wrenched on the tail, tugging backwards, his muscles bulging, his face flushed.

A loud snort issued from the mutant, and the creature halted and tilted its head to one side, attempting to glimpse the strange being that seemed determined on strangling its tail.

Blade felt the tail ripple and flex, and then he nearly lost his grip as the beast tried to flick him off. He dug his nails into the mutation's skin and his knees and boots into the soil.

The monster gurgled and blinked, and without any warning whatsoever, as if the weight of the seven-foot giant on its tail barely bothered it, the creature resumed walking toward the spring.

Dear Spirit, no! Blade's mind screamed. He could think of nothing else to do to slow the beast, so he did the only thing he could despite the revulsion he felt; he leaned down, opened wide, and sank his strong teeth into the leathery flesh.

Screeching shrilly, the mutant let go of Zed and turned, bending on itself, twisting its body nearly in half, exhibiting a remarkable dexterity and elasticity. It roared and snapped at the Warrior.

Blade saw the maw swooping at him, and he released the tail and rolled backwards, covering eight feet before pushing to his knees.

The creature came after him!

Blade scrambled backward, narrowly evading a second snap, surprised at the burst of speed the beast displayed. His left hand slipped and he went down on his back, and in that instant the mutant loomed above him, breathing fetid breath in his face. He girded his legs to try to spring to the side, to safety.

"Get out of the way!" shouted a familiar voice, and the Kid was standing next to him, those Redhawks cocked and ready. Four shots boomed, and the gunfighter sent two rounds into each protruding eye.

Blade rolled to the left and shoved erect, and as he did his hands came in contact with a metallic object. He glanced down to discover the Mossberg. In pure reflex he swept the shotgun to his shoulder and pumped off three shots, aiming at the mutant's neck. The buckshot sent flesh and fluid flying.

Hissing like a snake, the creature tried to retreat into the brush.

More guns were added to the fray. Brount emptied his pistols into the monster. Many of the hired guns did likewise. The withering volley lasted for half a minute.

"Die!" the Kid yelled.

Ever so slowly, its purple tongue extended past its lips, the mutation sank to the earth. A brackish substance oozed from the corners of its mouth, and it convulsed, its skin rippling and quivering.

Blade darted forward, skirting the squat, odious bulk, and ran to Zed.

The bodyguard lay on his back, his eyes closed, breathing shallowly. His left arm had been broken at the elbow, and the bone had torn through the skin. Blood flowed from an awful gash on the right side of his head. The worst wound, by far, was the damage done to his stomach, where the mutant had taken a bite out of his body, exposing Zed's intestines and internal organs.

"No!" Blade moaned, and sank to his knees. He reached out and felt Zed's right wrist for a pulse and found a weak heartbeat. "No!"

To the Warrior's astonishment, Zed's eyes flickered open. "Blade? Is that you?"

"I'm here," Blade confirmed, taking the bodyguard's hand in his own.

"I'm so cold."

"I'll go find a coat or blanket," Blade proposed.

"No!" Zed declared. "Don't leave. I don't have much time left."

Blade closed his eyes and his chin sagged onto his chest.

"I'm sorry," Zed said softly.

The Warrior looked at him. "What in the world for?"

"I won't be able to help you when it will matter the most," Zed mentioned wistfully.

Ineffable sadness filled the Warrior.

"Sorry we got off on the wrong foot," Zed remarked, his voice becoming ever weaker. "I've liked having you as a friend." He paused. "You are my friend, aren't you?"

"I'm your friend."

Zed smiled.

Blade realized the others were gathered around, watching in somber silence. He saw the Kid to his left, and nearby stood Brount with his brow knit.

Maddie materialized on the right and knelt alongside the Warrior. "Zed?"

"Maddie? Is that you?" Zed asked, craning his neck. "I feel like I'm in a tunnel."

"I—I—" Maddie said, and broke off, sobbing.

"Don't cry, Maddie," Zed urged. A thought seemed to strike him and he started. "Did you get the thing that killed me?"

"We took care of it," Blade said.

"Thanks," Zed stated, and grinned wanly. "What a way to go, huh? Chomped by a big, ugly toad! Who would have figured—" He inhaled deeply and loudly, then abruptly ceased breathing.

"Zed!" Maddie wailed.

Blade heard footsteps, and Daniel Brount spoke from directly behind them, a patronizing remark that made Blade want to leap up and pound the man senseless and filled the Warrior with a profound animosity for the ruler of Shantytown.

"That's funny. I didn't know you two were so attached to the moron."

CHAPTER FOURTEEN

From afar the Union headquarters appeared to consist of a ring of towering gravel mounds.

"This place was called a gravel pit before the war," Brount explained as the column neared the mounds from the north. "The gravel was used in constructing roads and buildings, I believe."

"Why was this spot selected for the headquarters?" Blade inquired.

"Can you think of a better-camouflaged site?"

"No," Blade confessed, marveling at the ingeniousness of whoever had concocted the idea in the distant past. To the casual observer the gravel pit would be uninteresting or perhaps slightly sinister, hardly a spot worthy of investigation. No one would suspect the central core of the Union's evil, minor empire flourished at such a dismal spot.

"We're being watched right now," Brount disclosed. "There are lookouts posted on the top of each mound, and they can see for miles in all directions."

Another strategic plus. Blade perceived he had better not underestimate his adversaries. In addition to being heartless murderers, petty tyrants, and ruthless racketeers, they were devious and resourceful.

"Crusher will probably sent out a welcoming committee," Brount mentioned.

"The friendly sort, is he?" Blade quipped.

A tremendous, metallic roar rent the cool, early afternoon air, increasing in volume, and from a gap between two mounds on the east shot a succession of noisy vehicles, eight in all, five cars and three pickup trucks. Their motors created a raucous din as they accelerated and bore down on the column of wagons and riders. All of the vehicles rattled and clanked, and all were in need of a paint job. Several lacked windshields, and one of the pickup trucks had a hood missing.

Blade studied them closely as they approached. Each vehicle had undergone extensive modification. Although at first glance they presented the illusion of being dilapidated and on the verge of collapse, in actuality they were makeshift tanks. Heavy armor plating had been applied to the sides and the grill of each one. Wire mesh covered all the windows. Square openings had been cut in the roofs of the five cars directly above the rear seat, enabling a man to stand on the back seat of each, his upper torso visible over the car from the waist up. Each man held a machine gun. There were also two armed men in the bed of each pickup.

The vehicles bore to the right, swinging around the column in a wide circle, the drivers and machine gunners whooping and hollering. Many of Brount's hired killers returned the yells and cheers.

"We'll party hearty tonight," Brount said, raising his voice to be heard above the racket.

"I've always wanted to attend a party held at a gravel pit," Blade cracked. "For entertainment we can sit around and throw gravel at one another."

Brount laughed. "You're in for a real treat. Few people have ever seen what lies on the other side of those mounds."

"More mounds?" Blade joked, hoping his false, light-hearted attitude would conceal his true feelings toward the man. Putting a smile on his face when he really despised the man wasn't easy.

"You'll see," Brount said, chuckling.

They rode into the gap through which the vehicles had appeared. Blade craned his neck and spotted the lookouts. He shifted his attention to the dirt road ahead, remembering the description Maddie had provided of the headquarters, thinking he was prepared for anything. But the spectacle that spread before his astounded gaze as they emerged from between the gravel mounds dazzled him.

Who would have imagined!

An oasis bloomed in the five-acre area encompassed by the mounds. Fertile topsoil had long ago been deposited on the surface and seeded, resulting in a spacious expanse of grass watered by an elaborate irrigation system from a well. Although it was only late March, the grass already was a light shade of green. In the middle of the area a half-acre pond added a pristine touch to the landscape. North of the pond stood a magnificent mansion, three stories in height, in superb condition. And the entire structure had been recently painted. Behind the edifice were two other buildings.

The road slanted to the front of the mansion, then widened into a paved parking lot situated to the west of the manor.

Blade's eyes widened when they saw the three machines at rest in the parking lot. "I don't believe it!" he exclaimed.

"Have you ever seen anything like them?" Brount asked proudly.

"Never," Blade confessed.

They were like gargantuan mechanical dinosaurs, three incredible postwar juggernauts ready to devour or crush at the flick of a switch or the wrench of a gear. All three were painted a bright yellow, and each was obviously maintained in as superb a shape as possible. The largest of the trio reared 50 feet into the air at its apex. Enormous treads provided the means of locomotion. A rectangular cabin, indented in the center, was perched atop the tread wheels, and from this cabin rose a towering beam or girder to which cables were attached. Another, smaller, girder hung from the tip of the first, and at the end of the smaller girder an immense metal mouth or scoop, designed with three spiked teeth on each lip, completed the contrivance.

Brount noticed the direction of the Warrior's gawking gaze and snickered. "They were used as construction equipment once. That big sucker was called an excavator or a steam shovel or some such bullshit."

Next to the steam shovel was a jumbo tractorlike vehicle with an open cab, black treads, and at the front end a mammoth, concave blade.

"The second one there was known as a bulldozer," Brount said.

Last in the row came an elephantine truck. An arrow-shaped scoop, three times the height of an average man, tapered backwards from the front of the grill. A raised bed or holding container comprised the rear two-thirds. The tires were stupendous.

"What was the third one used for?" Blade queried.

"I think it was used for plowing snow," Brount disclosed.

"And now?"

"If you're lucky, Crusher may give you a demonstration," Brount responded.

Over three dozen people were milling outside the mansion, and half were women in bright dresses. Two figures detached themselves from the crowd and came to greet the column.

"Be on your best behavior," Brount warned. "Here comes Crusher and his right-hand man, Pelczar."

Blade studied them intently. Neither were what he expected. The name Crusher Payne had conjured an image of an uncouth Neanderthal who belched every two minutes and dispensed mayhem with single-minded abandon. Blade's preconception, however, couldn't have been further from the truth.

The taller of the pair stood well over six feet in height, a leonine, virile man in a blue suit who radiated authority and walked with a stately bearing. His gray hair was slicked back from his forehead. Blue eyes regarded the world with a disturbing severity. His pointed chin accented his harsh features.

The second man wore a brown suit, and his stocky frame seemed about to burst the garment at the seams. He trailed the first man by a yard, his large hands hanging near the open flaps of his jacket. Curly brown hair framed a square, lined face.

"Crusher!" Brount declared to the man in blue. "Nice to see you again."

"Same here," Crusher Payne replied offhandedly in a low voice, his eyes on the wagons now entering the central area.

"Hello, Pelczar," Brount said to the second man, who merely nodded.

"What's with all the wagons? Are you evacuating Shantytown?" Crusher Payne asked.

Brount cackled while dismounting. "No. I've brought you a surprise."

Crusher scrutinized the riders and nodded at Kid Zanto. "How's it going, Kid?"

"Can't complain," the gunfighter replied.

"I don't see Arnie with you," Crusher observed.

"He's dead," Brount divulged.

"Damn. Arnie was a good man. How'd he die?"

Brount pointed at Blade. "He killed him."

"Oh?" Crusher Payne responded, staring at the Warrior. "Isn't he new?"

"Yeah. I'd like you to meet my new second in command, Blade," Brount said, introducing him.

The Warrior slid to the ground and offered his right hand to Payne. "I'm pleased to meet you."

"Are you?" Crusher asked, and shook.

The strength in Payne's grip surprised Blade. Under the blue suit, Blade deduced, must be layers of muscle. "I've heard a lot about you."

"Nothing good I hope," Crusher said. "So you're

Brount's new second in command. What happened to Butch?"

"He's dead," Brount disclosed.

"How'd *he* die?"

"Blade wasted him."

Crusher Payne's forehead furrowed in bewilderment. "You killed Butch too?"

"Afraid so," Blade admitted.

"Do you go around killing people for the fun of it?" Crusher inquired facetiously.

"They rubbed me the wrong way."

"Uh-huh." Crusher surveyed the riders again. "And where's Zed? No. Let me guess."

"He's dead," Brount revealed.

Crusher Payne looked at the Warrior in astonishment. "Not you *again*?"

"I can't claim the credit for Zed. I liked him. A mutant killed him yesterday," Blade explained. "I tried to save him."

"What a rotten way to buy the farm," Crusher stated. "I hate those frigging mutants. One killed my father."

The revelation stunned Blade. He peered at the Union leader with renewed interest. "A mutant killed my father too."

"Fascinating," Payne said, and glanced at Brount. "Have your men take their horses to the stables, and then they can join the festivities. I brought in some foxes from Trego for the night, and later we're having roast pig. The brew is on me."

"As usual, your generosity is overwhelming," Brount said.

"Don't brown-nose me, Dan," Crusher snapped. "You know better." He gazed at the wagons. "So what's the big surprise?"

"We ran into an old friend of yours a couple of days ago," Brount mentioned.

"Who?"

"Harland Warner."

Crusher Payne stiffened and scowled. "Warner! That bastard! I hope you gave him a taste of his own medicine."

A self-satisfied smirk creased Brount's countenance. "We did better than that. Warner won't ever bother you again."

"You mean . . . ?" Crusher queried hopefully.

"The son of a bitch is history."

"Who got him? You? The Kid?" Crusher wanted to know. He paused and stared at Blade. "Don't tell me."

"Yep," the Warrior said.

A sincere smile curled Payne's mouth upward. "I owe you a debt of gratitude. Warner caused us more grief than I care to remember. The man was number one on my hit list, and I tried over a dozen times to have the sucker snuffed. This is terrific news."

"Glad I could make your day."

"And I'm glad you don't confine your killing activities to our men," Crusher joshed.

"Before you become all misty eyed, you should take a look in the four flatbeds," Brount advised.

"What's in them?"

"I think you should see for yourself."

"Okay," Crusher said, and nodded at Blade and the Kid. "Why don't you mingle? Grab a drink. Talk to the ladies, or whatever else you might . . ." He suddenly stopped, his eyes locked on something or someone behind them.

A moment later Maddie Stender joined them. "Hello," she said, greeting Payne.

"Danny, where did you find this vision of loveliness?" Crusher inquired in a gentlemanly, urbane tone. "Have you been hiding her somewhere?" He took Maddie's right hand in his and raised her knuckles to his lips. "Your beauty, my dear, and I trust you won't mind if I speak frankly, is exquisite."

Blade saw a crimson tinge creep into Daniel Brount's cheeks, and he noticed the man seemed to have difficulty in speaking because Brount cleared his throat twice.

"Crusher, I'd like you to meet Maddie Stender. She works for me at the Booze N' Broads."

"So lovely a woman working in such a hovel?" Crusher said, bestowing a kingly smile on the lady in question.

"Please, Mister Payne," Maddie responded self-consciously. "You're embarrassing me."

Crusher adopted a horrified expression and reluctantly released her hand. "I would never dream of causing you discomfort. So ravishing a woman should always be treated with the utmost courtesy."

"Are you always so gallant?" Maddie responded.

"A natural reaction to the delight of making your acquaintance," Crusher answered, laying on the charm. "I insist on having you as my personal guest of honor during your stay here. Perhaps I might even be able to entice you to stay."

Blade placed his left hand over his mouth so no one would see his ear-to-ear smile at the sight of Daniel Brount's anguished visage. Brount looked like a man who had just had a broomstick shoved down his throat.

"I only came because Mister Brount needed a cook," Maddie stated.

"Then my eternal gratitude to Danny's taste buds," Crusher declared in a patently romantic fashion. He glanced at Brount and did a double take. "What's wrong with you? You look sick?"

"I'm not feeling well," Brount conceded in a raspy tone.

Blade thought he would burst out laughing.

"Well, let's attend to your surprise and then you can rest while I give Maddie the grand tour," Crusher said, and beamed at her. "It is all right if I call you Maddie, isn't it?"

"Sure."

"And you may call me Crusher."

Pretending to be intriqued by one of the eastern mounds, Blade turned away and coughed to relieve the ticklish sensation in his throat.

"Why don't you go with the Kid and Blade. Have fun," Crusher went on. "I'll be with you as soon as I've conducted some business with Dan."

"No rush," Maddie said.

"There is where I'm concerned," Crusher said sweetly.

Kid Zanto walked toward the crowd. "Let's find me a drink," he declared.

The Warrior and Maddie strolled after the youth. She leaned close to the giant and made a snorting sound.

"Do you believe that jerk?"

"I thought you were falling for his garbage," Blade commented.

"Credit me with more intelligence, please."

"Sorry. Did you see Brount's face?"

"Yeah, and I loved every minute of it," Maddie said.

"You'd better be careful," Blade advised. "If you try to play those two against each other, you'll be playing with fire."

She looked him in the eyes and grinned. "You're a fine one to talk. I have a fair idea of what you're up to, remember?"

"So?"

"So by the time you're through, I expect they'll convert this gravel pit into a cemetery."

CHAPTER FIFTEEN

The party was in full swing 30 minutes later.

After the greetings were out of the way and Crusher's men had welcomed their pals in Brount's organization, everyone ventured indoors. A spacious, plush room located to the right of the front entrance accommodated everybody with space to spare. Trays of bite-sized sandwiches covered over half of the counter on the bar running the entire length of the north wall. Copious quantities of liquor were being consumed at a prodigious rate, as if those doing the imbibing anticipated never being able to drink again and wanted to insure their last binge was the binge to end all binges. Laughter and bawdy talk filled the air. The ladies from Trego demonstrated a remarkable flair for inducing relaxation in the men.

Blade, Maddie, and the Kid stood to one side of the festivities, near the west wall within a yard of the doorway, and watched the celebration.

"And you say they do this at every conference?" Blade said to Kid Zanto.

"Every time," the youth confirmed.

"I'm surprised they don't make the meetings monthly

instead of bimonthly,'' Blade quipped.

''*I'm* surprised Crusher Payne isn't here pawing all over me,'' Maddie said. ''I must be losing my touch.''

''You want him to paw all over you?'' Blade asked in disbelief.

''Of course not. But's its bad for a woman's ego to have a man drooling over her one minute and ignoring her the next.''

''I saw Crusher and Danny over by the flatbeds,'' the Kid mentioned. ''Crusher looked like he was about to lay an egg. I never saw the guy so mad.''

''What's up, do you think?'' Maddie queried.

''I'm sure we'll find out,'' Blade said, and glanced at the doorway. No guards were anywhere in evidence, and the party-goers were too absorbed in their frolicking and fondling to pay any attention to him. ''I'll be back in a while,'' he said, and stepped toward the corridor.

''Where are you going?'' Maddie questioned.

''To check out the mansion.''

''You'd better not,'' the Kid warned. ''Crusher doesn't allow anyone above the first floor except for a few of his men. The upper floors are off limits to us.''

''He never told me,'' Blade said, and grinned and winked.

''I'll go with you,'' Maddie offered.

''No, you won't,'' Blade stated. ''You stay put in case Crusher returns to drool over you some more.''

''If you go upstairs, by all rights I'm supposed to report you,'' the Kid noted.

''Will you?''

''Nope. You're my friend, and I don't rat on friends.''

''Good,'' Blade said, smiling. ''Will you keep an eye on Maddie while I'm gone?''

''Sure.''

''I don't need a baby-sitter,'' Maddie remarked indignantly.

''No, but you need someone to wipe off the drool,'' Blade retorted, and walked into the hall. The corridor extended the width of the mansion, and a half-dozen doors opened onto it farther along. Paintings hung on the walls. Ornate light fixtures hung from the ceiling. Thick carpet covered the floor. In all respects the headquarters of the Union reeked of affluence, of the wealth of ill-gotten gains the Union had reaped over the decades since World War Three. Blade had witnessed the same pattern before. While the majority of the people residing in northern Wisconsin languished in abject poverty and endured an existence of shallow meaning and misery, those who oppressed the people lived in opulent luxury, glutting themselves at the expense of those who barely eked out a living.

All through history the same pattern had held true. Power-mongers, tyrants, dictators, intellectual elites, financial cartels, crime czars, burauratic sycophants, and other varieties of domineering, manipulative, autocratic individuals and groups would arise and subjugate the people militarily, morally, or economically, oppress the common citizens unmercifully and bleed them materially until the populace eventually arose in righteous fury and overthrew their tormentors. Later a new group would arise, and on and on the cycle went.

Blade thought of the many types of power-mongers he'd encountered in his travels, and he wondered how long it would be before the earth was finally rid of their blighting existence. The prospect of achieving genuine global peace seemed as remote now as it had been prior to the war, perhaps more so. He shook his head, derailing his train of thought, and concentrated on the matter at hand.

A third of the way along the corridor, on the left, a stairway spiraled up to the second floor. He padded down the hall, his boots sinking almost soundlessly in the luxurious carpet, and paused at the base of the stairs. A quick glance insured no one else had stepped into the corridor, and he quickly ran up the stairs to find another lavishly adorned hallway and another series of doors.

Blade ran to the first door on the right and threw it wide. Beyond was a richly decorated bedroom containing a king-sized bed and polished mahogany furniture. Disappointed, he went to the next door and discovered a similar bedroom. He wanted to find an office, a file room, or a supply room, something to give him more insight into the Union's activities.

On an impulse he returned to the stairwell and ascended to the third floor, halting on the landing when he heard the buzz of subdued voices coming from the right. He held the Mossberg strap tightly with his left hand to prevent the shotgun from flapping on his back as he tiptoed to a partially open door ten feet away. A mere crack separated the jamb from the door, and he put his left ear to the crack to listen. The words he heard immediately piqued his interest.

"—know about this guy? How the hell could you appoint him as your second in command without checking him out?"

Blade recognized the irate speaker as Crusher Payne.

"Give me a break, Crusher. How many of your men turned in a complete background history before you hired them?" Daniel Brount countered.

"I don't like it," Crusher declared. "There's something about the guy. I know I've heard his name before, but I can't remember where."

"Strange," Brount commented. "I had the same feeling, like I should know him, or know of him."

"Didn't it strike you as the least bit suspicious that he snuffed Arnie and Butch?" Crusher inquired.

"Hey, I was there when both went down. Their deaths didn't appear to be premeditated."

"For all you know the guy might have been waiting for the least little provocation to blow them away," Crusher said. "I don't believe their deaths were a coincidence. You just got through telling me this Blade was supposed to fight Zed to the death, and then refused to kill Zed when he had the chance. Why not? If he's so touchy about being rubbed the wrong way, why did he allow Zed to live?"

"I never thought of it that way."

"You'd better *start* thinking. Get your butt in gear. I

appointed you as one of my lieutenants because I believed you were sharp and could handle the job, but if you've made a major mistake I'll begin to have my doubts."

There was silence for several seconds.

"I'll find out if Blade is up to something. I promise," Brount vowed.

"And I'll hold you to it," Crusher said. "I have too much going on right now to be able to devote any time to this Blade. Thanks for sending the messenger on ahead to let us know you were coming several days early. I had time to prepare the reception, and I've sent riders to all the other lieutenants instructing them to be here by tomorrow night or else."

"What do you make of the gun business?"

"If I'm right, we've been double-crossed, and no one double-crosses us and gets away with it."

"What can we do?"

"Teach them respect."

"Isn't that dangerous?"

"Not if they want to do business in our region. Their delegation is due to arrive on the day originally slated as the beginning of the conference. Since we'll have our men here ahead of time, we can arrange a suitable reception."

"We'll be taking a big risk. They're not to be trifled with."

"Neither are we!" Crusher snapped.

"Why would they do it? Doesn't make sense," Brount said.

"Who knows? They probably figured we'd never catch on. They took us for a bunch of chumps. They'll learn the hard way we're not."

Blade heard the sound of papers being shuffled.

"Say, Crusher?"

"What?"

"I need to talk to you about Maddie," Brount declared.

"She's a fox, Dan. I'm surprised you haven't claimed her for yourself."

"I have."

Another silence persisted for 15 seconds.

"You don't say," Crusher Payne said slowly.

"She's special to me," Brount stated. "I mean *really* special. I intend to marry her."

"What the hell for? You can have the pick of any woman you want? Why tie yourself to one snatch?"

"Ever since I laid eyes on her, she's the only woman I've wanted. I hired her so I could watch over her and insure no one else put the moves on her, and I think I was making headway until a jerk named Vern Feldman came along and tried to sweet-talk his way into her pants. I tried to warn him off, but the asshole wouldn't listen. So I went out to his farm and had Arnie and Butch hold his arms while I pounded him to a pulp," Brount detailed, and laughed. "Since then, I've been biding my time with Maddie, waiting for her to warm to me."

"Why bother?" Crusher Payne asked. "Just rape the bitch and be done with it."

"I can't, Crusher. I won't. I think I love her."

"She means nothing to me. If you want her, you can have her. I learned a long time ago that a man can't ever trust a woman. They're only good for two things, balling and cooking. Maddie is a prime piece, but snatches are a dime a dozen."

"Thanks," Brount said softly.

"Hey, we're friends, aren't we? And friends stick together. Falling out over a lousy broad would be stupid."

"I agree."

"Does she suspect you killed Feldman?"

"I doubt it. I had the story spread that scavangers were responsible. She'll never learn the truth, just like the Kid will never learn the truth about his dad."

"Too bad the old fool couldn't see things your way. Those so-called decent schmucks are always the most hardheaded."

"Don't I know it! I tried to reason with the man, but Zanto refused to allow his son to come work for me. I'd seen the Kid practice, and I knew there were few his equal. I offered to pay Old Man Zanto, but he declined. The only way his son would work for the likes of me, he claimed, was over his dead body,'' Brount recollected, and snickered. ''That was easily arranged.''

''Some people are so obstinate it's unbelievable,'' Crusher mentioned. ''And it's always the honest putz who gives us all the aggravation. Why can't they—''

Blade suddenly tensed, intuitively aware he wasn't alone. He whirled, reaching for his right Bowie, expecting to find Pelczar or another of Crusher's men.

Instead, there stood the Kid a foot off, his face a scarlet hue, his lips twitching in suppressed fury, his hands resting on the Redhawks, his fiery eyes on the door.

In a rush of insight Blade perceived the youth had overheard Brount's remarks, and he lunged, wrapping his left arm around the Kid's waist and clamping his right hand on the gunfighter's mouth. He strained and lifted the Kid bodily, then hastened toward the stairwell.

Thrashing and kicking, the Kid attempted to break free. Muffled words came in a jumble and he tried to wrench his mouth loose.

''Behave!'' Blade said sternly, and carted his burden down the stairs to the next floor, where he dashed into the first bedroom he'd visited earlier and kicked the door shut. ''I won't release you if you don't calm down,'' he threatened.

Kid Zanto was not about to calm down. He bucked and struggled, and even endeavored to bite the Warrior's right hand, in an effort to disengage himself.

''I'll tie you up and stuff you in a closet,'' Blade admonished. ''Get a grip on yourself.''

The Kid's blue eyes still blazed a red-hot rage, but he ceased battling and held his body stiffly.

''All right. Don't do anything foolish,'' Blade said, and released the youth.

''I thought you were my friend!'' Kid Zanto exploded, his whole body shaking, his ire boiling over.

''I am.''

''The hell you are! You stopped me from going in there

and killing the son of a bitch who murdered my dad!'' the Kid declared loudly.

''Keep your voice down or they'll hear you.''

''Who cares?'' the Kid snapped.

''You should. So now you know what I've suspected all along. You know Brount for the worthless slime he is, and you rightfully want to avenge the death of your father. But if you had stormed into that room just now, you would have thrown your life away. Oh, you would have challenged Brount and probably killed him, but Crusher or his bodyguard, Pelczar, who was most likely also inside, would have gunned you down in return. And then what would you have accomplished?''

''Do you expect me to do nothing?''

''No. But I expect you to bide your time and strike when the circumstances are favorable. For reasons I can't explain, I want to see Brount planted six feet under too. We can work together if you'll rein in your temper. Give me time to formulate a plan.''

The Kid digested the proposal sullenly and finally nodded. ''Okay. I'll hold back for now. But I won't wait long! If you don't come up with a humdinger of a plan soon, I'll go after Brount on my own, and nothing you can say or do will stop me the next time.'' So saying, the youth spun and stalked from the room.

Blade placed his hands on his hips and sighed. Why did he have the feeling this was the calm before the storm?

CHAPTER SIXTEEN

The next day passed uneventfully for the Warrior.

All of Brount's men spent the night in a long, low building situated to the rear of the mansion and adjoining the horse stables. Each of them was assigned a green cot, and Blade tossed fitfully on his, unable to sleep soundly, too worried about Maddie to relax. Crusher had allotted her a room in the mansion, and Blade spent the night envisioning her being assaulted by Brount or Payne. In the morning he sought her out and discovered she had not been molested. She had, in fact, slumbered like the proverbial baby.

During the forenoon hours Blade amused himself by watching the Union members shuffle about the headquarters, treading lightly, their expressions pained at the slightest loud noise. Most had drunk to excess, but by noon they were sufficiently recovered to begin drinking anew.

The Kid kept to himself most of the day, rarely speaking to anyone, and snapping at those who intruded on his reflection.

Once Brount approached the Warrior and asked if Blade knew the reason for the Kid's unusual behavior.

"Nope," Blade had fibbed. "Maybe he misses Susie."

"Only an idiot gets stuck on a woman," Brount had complained, and waltzed off.

Leaving Blade to contemplate the state of Daniel's Brount's intellect. The Warrior intentionally refrained from snooping about the mansion or the grounds. In the afternoon he strolled over to the parking lot and admired the construction machinery and the cars and pickups. As he gazed up at the steam shovel, marveling at its size, he glimpsed Crusher Payne and Brount watching him from a second floor mansion window. He studiously ignored them and continued walking around the machines and inspected the massive tires and other features. When next he casually gazed at the mansion, Payne and Brount were gone.

Early evening brought the second of Crusher's lieutenants to the gravel pit, a portly man accompanied by 12 hired guns. An hour later the next arrived, and by nine o'clock that night all seven of the lieutenants were present and the ranks of the killers had swelled to 104, not including Payne's three dozen men.

Blade stood outside the mansion, near the front entrance, and observed the Union members who were congregating between the manor and the pond. He realized Crusher Payne now had a small army at his disposal, and fully understood why no one had arisen to defy the Union in over one hundred years. Few were the powers that could field a force large enough to defeat the Union. The Freedom Federation could, but he was loathe to return to the Home and formally petition the Family's allies for aid, especially when he was already on the scene and might be able to throw a monkey wrench into the works on his own.

A second night of partying occurred, even rowdier than the previous night. Crusher Payne had several dozen women brought in from Trego. Upon questioning one of the killers, Blade discovered where, exactly, the women came from: Payne operated a house of prostitution in Trego, widely considered to be the largest in the land.

On the second morning of the Warrior's stay at the gravel pit, Crusher Payne called a mass meeting on the ground in front of the mansion. Orders were issued, and the seven lieutenants were each given a specific task to perform.

The tasks lent themselves to speculation. A ditch five feet high and three feet wide, aligned parallel to the pond and within ten feet of the water, was dug by crews working in shifts and completed in one day. Trenches were excavated halfway up each gravel mound. A machine gun, a 50-caliber, was mounted on the mansion roof. Automatic rifles were propped alongside every window.

One fact became apparent to Blade. The Union was preparing for a war. Crusher Payne had laid a trap for someone. The ditch and the new trenches could conceal over half of Payne's army, and anyone caught on the open ground separating the mansion and the pond would be hard pressed to escape the headquarters alive. The men in the trenches on the eastern mounds would render retreat nearly impossible.

That night there was no partying. The prostitutes had been shuttled to Trego in the pickups and cars during the day. An atmosphere of tense expectancy seized the men, and few joked and laughed.

Blade and the Kid were standing close to the ditch, idly gazing at the pond, when footsteps sounded to their rear.

"You two must be beat. I saw you digging a trench on one of the mounds this afternoon."

The Warrior turned, smiling. "Where have you been all day, Maddie? We haven't seen much of you today."

She stretched and stared at the stars overhead. "Brount has been spoiling me rotten. He's assigned a woman to wait on me hand and foot. My every wish is his command." She snickered. "The scumbucket."

Kid Zanto, who had hardly said a word all day, glanced at her and frowned. "He hasn't touched you, has he?" the gunfighter demanded harshly.

Maddie shook her head vigorously. "No, Kid, he hasn't

laid a hand on me. If he tries, I'll come running to you."

"You do that," the Kid said, and those three words implied a horrible fate was in store for Daniel Brount if he tried.

"I came out here to warn you," Maddie said to Blade.

"About what?" the Warrior responded.

"You might already know, but Crusher is expecting company tomorrow. I don't know who it is, but he's gearing up for trouble," Maddie said.

"I deduced as much."

"I heard Crusher and Brount talking. Payne is hot under the collar about someone misleading him. He's spoiling for a fight, if I'm any judge of his character."

"Tomorrow promises to be a lively day," Blade remarked.

"Take care of yourself," Maddie told him.

The Warrior looked at the Kid. "Do you mind if I say a few words to Maddie in private?"

"Your business is your affair," replied the youth, and he ambled in the direction of the manor.

"What's up?" Maddie inquired when the Kid was out of earshot.

"The Kid told me you were the one who persuaded him to go upstairs after me the other night."

"I did. So?"

"So I distinctly recall asking him to stay downstairs and watch over you."

Maddie shrugged. "I wasn't in any danger, and I was worried about you, so I talked him into going up."

"Why did you come on this trip?"

His blunt, unexpected query caught her off guard, and she blinked her eyes and swallowed before replying. "I thought you knew. I came because Brount offered me a bonus to do his cooking."

"What was the real reason?"

"I don't know what you mean."

"Don't you? Zed told me you came along to watch over me. The bonus was only part of the reason," Blade said.

"What if I did?" Maddie stated defensively. "We're

friends, and friends watch out for one another."

"I don't want you to place yourself in jeopardy again on account of me," Blade instructed her.

"I'm a free person and I'll do as I damn please," Maddie said testily.

"You'll get yourself killed."

"If I do, it's my decision," she said defensively.

Blade lowered his voice. "Please, Maddie. For me. I can't do what I have to do and watch over you too. You're impairing my effectiveness."

"Well, excuse me for living!" Maddie snapped, and turned on her heels and stormed off.

Terrific! Just what he needed! Blade shifted and focused on the surface of the pond. The only two people he could rely upon at the Union headquarters, and they were both in an emotional funk. The Kid's hot temper made him unreliable, and there was no predicting how long the youth would hold himself in check and refrain from gunning down Dan Brount. Revenge was all the Kid lived for, the supreme motivation in his life at the moment, and when the crunch came his performance might be erratic.

Maddie had not told the truth, Blade felt. Either he had gravely misjudged her, or her attraction for him went past friendship. She might have a crush on him, a crush that would make her heedless of her own safety when the final fight came. He racked his brain for an argument he could use to convince Brount to send her back to Shantytown, but viable ideas eluded him until he considered the obvious. A smile curled his mouth and he headed for the mansion, scouring the grounds for any sign of Brount.

"Hey, Blade!"

The Warrior halted, recognizing the hailer as Karl, the hired gun who invariably wore the buckskin shirt and green pants. "Yes?"

Karl walked up and looked around, then spoke. "Some of us have been wondering about the ditch and the trenches and all the rest. We're curious about what's going down."

"Understandable," Blade said.

"We figured you might know, being so close to Mister Brount and all, and we figured you'd be willing to tell us although no one else would," Karl disclosed.

"If I knew, I'd tell you," Blade stated. "But Brount hasn't said word one to me. Sorry."

Karl shrugged and walked to the right. "Oh, well. Thanks anyway. You're a stand-up kind of guy."

The Warrior resumed his hunt for Brount. So some of the men thought highly of him! While flattering and interesting, the news rated as irrelevant in light of his current predicament. He crossed the grass to the front entrance and went inside, where he saw the object of his search standing in the corridor at the base of the stairwell, conversing with the head of the Union. "Mister Brount, I need to have a few words with you."

They swung toward him, perplexed. Pelczar came through a door on the right side of the hall and joined them, as ever coiled like a spring and ready to pounce at the slightest provocation.

"What is it, Blade?" Brount responded, a tinge of nervousness in his tone.

"I want to talk to you about Maddie."

Brount and Crusher Payne exchanged glances.

"Oh?" Brount said.

"Yeah. I'm concerned about her."

"In what way?"

"As you know, the two of us are friends. And that's all we are. Friends. Period. And as her friend, I don't think she should be here tomorrow," Blade said.

"Why not?" Crusher Payne asked, interrupting.

"I'm not an idiot. You're preparing for serious trouble. If there's going to be a battle here, then this isn't the right place for Maddie to be. You've sent almost all the other women away, so why allow her to remain and expose her to danger?" Blade asked tactfully.

"She'll be in no danger," Crusher said.

"Can you guarantee she won't?"

Payne straightened and his hands clenched. "Are you doubting my word?"

"Never, Mister Payne," Blade said with the utmost civility. "If you say she's safe here, then she's safe. I merely wanted to satisfy my own mind."

"Now you know," Crusher snapped imperiously.

"My apologies for disturbing you," Blade said, then rotated and exited out the front door.

"He has a point," Brount declared.

"Don't start again."

"But I don't want any harm to come to Maddie."

Crusher Payne sighed and placed his right hand on his lieutenant's left shoulder. "You're trying my patience, Dan. We've been through this six times today. Maddie will be safe in the mansion. I'll appoint four men to guard her at all costs. We can't permit her to leave yet. I was all set to send her to Shantytown when you informed me last night that Blade and her are close friends. Now this confirms the way they feel. She's leverage, Dan, leverage we can use against the giant if he gives us any grief. She's a loaded gun pointed right at his head, and I think Blade knows it."

Brount frowned and kicked at the carpet. "I wish there was another way."

"There isn't," Crusher assured him, and looked at his personal bodyguard. "Pel, go check on Blade. Follow him until he turns in for the night. Let me know if he talks to anyone."

Pelczar nodded and trudged outdoors, pausing to allow his eyes to adjust to the dim light, his hands, as always, held near the open flaps of his coat. Under those flaps were the Desert Eagle .357 Magnum semiautomatic pistols he always carried, one in a black leather holster on each stocky hip. He scanned the grass for the giant, then turned to the right and walked around the mansion. As the chief enforcer for Crusher Payne, Pelczar was renowned for his tenacity and devotion to duty. Over four dozen opponents had fallen to his guns or his malletlike hands. He savored the fear he frequently saw in the faces of subordinates, and relished the dread he spread among those who lived under the iron Union rule. He viewed himself as the toughest man on two legs, and there were few who would dispute the contention.

He reached the northwest corner and halted.

Twenty feet distant were the giant and the punk gunman known as the Kid, and they appeared to be having a disagreement. Their words were too low to be heard.

Pelczar remained in the inky shadows and merely observed, his patience limitless, his body immobile. He saw the Kid start to head toward the mansion, but the giant grabbed the youth and a heated exchange followed.

"You can't stop me!" the Kid shouted.

"Now's not the time!" the giant responded.

Pelczar saw the giant remonstrate with the punk in a hushed tone, and minutes later they both went into the sleeping quarters. He waited for 15 minutes, until satisfied they had retired for the night, and then he retraced his route to the front entrance. He glanced at the gravel mounds, thinking of the bloodshed the new day would bring, and he smiled in eager anticipation. Spilling blood qualified as his favorite pastime. That, and busting heads and breaking bones and carving punks into itty-bitty pieces. He thought of the giant and the youth, and he hoped Crusher would allow him to snuff them. He disliked them both, particularly the giant. He wanted to wrap his thick fingers around the giant's throat and squeeze until the bastard's tongue turned purple. The prospect made him tingle.

CHAPTER SEVENTEEN

Perspiration caked his skin under his black leather vest.

The afternoon sun had driven the temperature up to an exceptional 72 degrees, the warmest day of the year so far. Blade stood at attention, his arms at his sides, the Mossberg slung over his left arm, a Mandall TAC-1 Carbine over his right arm, his gaze riveted to the gap in the eastern gravel mounds.

Where the blazes were they?

The day had commenced busily enough. All of the hired killers had been arranged in formation in front of the mansion first thing, and Payne had addressed them, informing them that there might be a battle before the day was done, explaining that someone—and he would not say who—had evidently attempted to swindle the Union. The guilty party or parties were due at the gravel pit before the end of the day. Payne gave an inspiring speech, urging his men to exhibit courage and loyalty to the Union, reminding them they were all members in the same organization and as such owed allegiance exclusively to one another.

After the speech weapons were dispersed and the disposition orders dispensed. One lieutenant and all his men were posted in the mansion and all the windows were opened, enabling them to fire at will when the time came. Three lieutenants, with all of their killers, filed into the new ditch and waited in hiding, sitting on the earthen floor. Two lieutenants were assigned the trenches on the mounds, and they strategically placed their men to afford the maximum firepower.

Crusher Payne's three dozen men were formed into a square formation of four even rows directly in front of the manor, their backs to the structure, their weapons slung over their shoulders.

Blade found himself, along with the 21 other men under Brount's command, lined up into one of two rows positioned near the parking lot. The rows ran at a 90-degree angle from the west end of Payne's formation so that the two forces were configured into half of a large rectangle. The ditch on the south completed the third side of the design, while the eastern row of gravel mounds constituted the fourth. Anyone who came into the headquarters area through the gap would be quite effectively, and literally, boxed in.

For hours the Union army waited, hot and restless under the sun.

The Warrior shifted his feet to insure the circulation wasn't impeded, then surveyed the area for the umpteenth time. He stood in the foremost row, at the north end, within a yard of Payne's men, who were on his left. To his right was the Kid, then the rest of the first row. Behind him was the second row of Brount's killers, while to their rear, facing eastward in the parking lot, were the armored cars and pickups and the heavy construction machinery.

All except for one vehicle. A solitary car had been sent out at daylight on an unknown mission and had yet to return.

As Blade watched and waited he came to several conclusions.

First, Crusher Payne must be worried about those who were due to arrive. The meticulous preparations indicated a potentially formidable adversary was expected, an adversary with devastating firepower of their own.

Second, fuel and spare parts for the construction machinery must be scarce. Why else would Payne have used the men to dig the ditch and the trenches when the steam shovel alone could have performed both tasks in a fraction of the time?

Third, Crusher Payne and Daniel Brount were up to something. Both had studiously avoided him all day, except when they gave him orders to carry out. They went out of their way to avoid giving the impression they were paying any attention to him. Strangely enough, Payne's personal bodyguard, the bullish Pelczar, constantly stared at the Warrior throughout the day, and once even grinned as if at a private joke.

Blade knew Maddie had not left. He'd glimpsed her several times at a third floor window. By all rights, if Brount cared for her as much as he claimed, she should have been sent home. There must be an ulterior motive accounting for her continued presence. But what? An uneasy feeling developed within him, and the apprehension grew as the day progressed. He was about to excuse himself on the pretext of going to the bathroom so he could seek out Maddie, when the strident roar of a racing motor arose from the east.

Instantly every man in the Union army tensed and focused on the opening between the eastern mounds.

Spewing dirt and stones from under its tires, the car sent off earlier returned, speeding toward where Crusher Payne and Brount stood side by side approximately ten yards from the Warrior.

The driver wheeled the armored vehicle in a tight curve and braked within six feet of the Union leader. He shouted through the mesh wiring covering his window. "They're about fifteen minutes behind me!"

Crusher Payne nodded. "Park with the rest. You know what to do."

With a curt nod the driver accelerated and drove toward the parking lot, compelling a half-dozen of Brount's men to scurry aside so he could reach his destination. Once the car had passed, the two lines reformed.

Payne raised his arms and yelled so all could hear. "Get ready, men! Check your weapons! The enemy is almost here!"

The enemy? What enemy? Blade wiped his brow with the back of his left hand and stared at the gap, eager to discover the identify of whoever had aroused Crusher Payne's wrath.

Brount came over. "Listen up!" he told his killers. "Watch for my signal. If I motion like this"—and he made a chopping movement with his right hand—"get the hell out of the way. The construction machinery and the other vehicles will come barreling through, and you'll be flattened like a pancake if you don't move your ass. Head toward the mansion and allow the vehicles to pass when I signal you. Any questions?"

None of his men spoke.

"Okay. Stay alert," Brount advised, and returned to Crusher's side.

Blade glanced at the mansion, but there was no sign of Maddie. He hoped she would have enough common sense to take shelter at the rear of the manor when the firing commenced.

The minutes dragged by.

Blade felt beads of sweat on his forehead, just under the hairline. He placed his weight on his right foot, then his left, flexing his leg muscles.

High overhead a hawk soared.

The Warrior worked his shoulders back and forth, limbering his neck and arms. From far off in the distance he heard the noise of approaching vehicles. Many vehicles. He placed his right hand on the strap to the Mandall.

Two minutes elapsed.

All eyes were on the gap in the eastern mounds when a brown military jeep drove into the central area and angled toward Crusher Payne. A second jeep followed, then a third. Next came two half-tracks. Then four troop transport trucks.

The convoy drove into the rectangle formed by the ditch and the Union men and came to a stop in the center, the lead jeep halting five yards from Crusher and Brount.

Blade gaped at the military vehicles, at the familiar red star adorning the doors of each, shocked by the sight of a Russian convoy so far north in Wisconsin.

The Russians!

The Union had dealings with the Russians!

During World War Three the Soviet Union had launched a two-pronged drive into the United States, with one prong landing on the Eastern seaboard and penetrating inland and the second sweeping across Alaska and down Canada towards the Western U.S. The coldest, harshest Canadian winter ever recorded did to the western prong what, centuries before, Russian winters had done to the Germans and Napoleon; the bitter weather demoralized and decimated their ranks, reducing the western prong to ruin and forcing them to retreat.

The Soviet advance in the eastern United States fared better. They took control of a belt of land stretching from New England into the deep South and west to the Mississippi River. Southern New York, southern Pennsylvania, Maryland, New Jersey, Kentucky, Virginia, West Virginia, and sections of North and South Carolina were subjugated. The Russians also dominated southern Ohio, southern Indiana, and portions of Illinois. But try as they might, they had been unable to expand the area under their rule in 106 years.

To find the Soviets in northern Wisconsin, hundreds of miles from their lines, staggered Blade. This meant they were actively engaged in activities designed to increase the geographic region under their thumb. They were on the move again. The leaders of the Freedom Federation must be warned! He resolved to do so at the first opportunity.

Russian soldiers clambered from the vehicles, all armed with slung AK-47's. Twenty emerged from each of the three foremost troop transports, and all 60 promptly assumed formation and stood at attention. Four Soviets climbed from each jeep. Six jumped down from the bed of each half-track. In short order 84 soldiers were in ranks six deep. Only the drivers remained in the half-tracks and the transport trucks.

A strutting Russian officer, attended by two subordinates, walked with clipped, precise steps over to Crusher Payne. Flamboyant medals decorated his chest. His black boots were polished to a sheen. A pistol snuggled in a flapped leather holster rested on his right hip. His crew-cut blond hair accented his angular visage. A cap, slanted at a cocky angle, perched on his head. "Ahhhh, my good friend, Crusher!" he declared loudly, stopping a pace from Payne and saluting as a token of his respect. "How pleasant to see you again."

The officer spoke perfect English without any trace of an accent, and Blade couldn't determine if the man was directly descended from the original occupation Russian stock or whether the officer was the result of the enforced impregnation program. In an effort to increase their dwindling numbers, after they had lost contact with the motherland and found themselves stranded without a hope of receiving periodic reinforcements, the Russians had instituted a program of impregnating selected American women. The offspring resulting from such unions were reared in special indoctrination camps. For three decades the Soviet breeding program had created citizens every bit as Russian as if they had been born and raised in the Soviet Union, and the officer in charge of the convoy could well be one.

"General Pronin," Crusher said coldly.

The officer seemed not to notice. He beamed and pointed at the fourth transport truck. "We have brought the weapons, as promised. An entire truckload of the latest automatics and semiautomatics we have manufactured."

"That's nice," Crusher said, an edge to his voice.

General Pronin blinked a few times, then glanced at his aides, both of whom were majors. "Is something wrong, friend Crusher?"

"You could say that."

"But what could it be?" Pronin responded, clearly bewildered. "We have arrived on the date specified, yes?"

"Yes."

"And we have brought the guns according to our arrangement, yes?"

"Evidently," Crusher said.

"Then I do not understand," General Pronin stated. "We are here at the right time with the weapons you ordered. You have graciously assembled your men to welcome us—"

"Sort of," Crusher said, interrupting.

"Sort of?" the Russian repeated, and his expression clouded. "Please, friend Crusher, do not beat around the bush. Why are you cross at us?"

Crusher Payne smirked and leaned closer until his nose almost touched the general's. "Does the name Harland Warner mean anything to you?"

General Pronin's mouth opened and closed. The question flustered him, and he took half a minute to regain control. "Yes," he said finally. "I know the name."

"I'll just bet you do!" Crusher snapped.

"What does Harland Warner have to do with our arrangement?" the officer inquired defensively.

"Everything!" Crusher exploded. "You lied to me!"

"I did not."

"Don't bullshit me!" Crusher declared angrily, jabbing his right thumb into the Russian's chest. "You went back on your word."

"How so?" General Pronin asked, his gaze straying to the Union forces to his right and straight ahead. He looked to the left and noticed the new ditch, then casually scrutinized the gravel mounds. Alarm flitted across his features.

"What were the conditions of our agreement?" Crusher queried.

"You know them as well as I do."

"Humor me, friend General," Crusher said. "What were they?"

General Pronin cleared his throat. "We agreed to provide you with a truckload of weapons every two months. In exchange, you are to give us sixty percent of the profits you reap on their sale."

"Go on," Crusher goaded.

"Pardon?" General Pronin replied, his forehead furrowed.

"What's the rest of it?"

"That, essentially, is our agreement," General Pronin insisted.

"Not by a long shot, it isn't," Crusher stated, and slapped his right thigh in frustration.

"Those were the details," Pronin said.

"You're forgetting something," Crusher said. "We agreed to be the exclusive supplier of your weapons in this region."

"So?"

The next words came out of Crusher like they were bursting from a cannon. "So why the hell did you have the same arrangement with Warner?"

"Who said we did?"

"Don't jerk me around, General!" Crusher warned. "Why else would Warner have wagonloads of the same types of weapons you supply? I'll tell you why! You made the same deal with Warner that you made with me, and I'll bet you've made the deal with others. You've promised all of us exclusive rights to the guns you sell, and then you go and furnish the guns to anyone and everyone."

"You misunderstand."

"Enlighten me, damn you!" Crusher stated.

"I will admit we furnished guns to Harland Warner, but we did not violate the terms of our agreement with you."

"The hell you didn't!"

"Please, calm down and I will explain," General Pronin offered. He turned and quickly whispered a few words to one of his aides, who then hastened to the Russian ranks near the convoy vehicles and whispered in the ear of a captain.

"I'm listening," Crusher said.

"We promised you exclusive rights in this area, in the

region you control, but we did not promise you exclusive rights to all of North America,'' General Pronin explained, his tone tinged by subtle sarcasm.

''Don't be a smart-ass.''

''I'm merely releating the facts. Yes, we entered into an agreement with you. And yes, we also entered into an agreement with Warner, but he was supposed to conduct his trade outside of your seven territories. If he violated the terms, the fault is not ours.''

''The hell it isn't!'' Crusher snapped. ''Exclusive rights to your weapons. Those were your exact words, you miserable son of a bitch.''

General Pronin's face became beet red. ''There is no need to be insulting, friend Crusher.''

''Nobody tries to pull a fast one on the Union, General,'' Crusher Payne declared somberly. ''Those weapons in the wrong hands could upset the balance of power in this region. You know that. And yet you're practically handing the damn guns out to any sucker who asks for them.'' He paused. ''I think you have something up your sleeve.''

The Russian glanced down at his coat sleeves. ''I assure you I do not.''

''Well, I do, friend General,'' Crusher said, and raised his right arm. ''Mess with us, will you?'' he challenged, and streaked his arm downward.

All hell broke loose.

CHAPTER EIGHTEEN

Had the Union forces opened fire at the moment the Russian soldiers emerged from the convoy vehicles, they undoubtedly would have defeated the Soviets expeditiously and with relatively few losses. But by waiting, by allowing the Soviet general to become suspicious and to alert his men, the Union lost the element of complete surprise. So when Crusher Payne's right arm swept down and the Union men grabbed at their weapons and opened fire, the Russians immediately returned the fire and a general battle ensued.

Blade hit the dirt, diving to the ground and rolling to the left, removing himself as a target.

The Kid did the same.

The chattering of automatic and semiautomatic rifles, the blasting of machine guns, the thundering of rifles and revolvers and pistols, the screams of the hit and the wails of the dying all rose in a clashing cacophony, a deafening din of immeasurable magnitude.

Blade saw Union killers and Russians dropping in heaps. Payne's men advanced toward the convoy, firing furiously. The Union men in the ditch rose up and cut loose, as did the men posted in the trenches on the gravel mounds.

Although the Russian soldiers were caught in the open, their vehicles afforded a small degree of shelter from the hail of lead directed at them. Troopers managed to climb into the half-tracks and unlimber the 50-caliber mounted machine guns in both vehicles. One of the half-track gunners took out an entire trench of Union men with a short, sustained burst. Hand grenades sailed through the air to explode among the Union forces, and shrieks and cries punctuated the explosions as torsos and limbs were torn asunder.

In the swirl of combat, with men running every which way, and the shooting and the blasts and the screams adding to the confusion, Blade lost track of Crusher Payne and Brount. He saw the gunman named Karl take a round in the throat and topple to the grass. Once he glanced at the Kid, feeling surprised the youth wasn't in the thick of things. His surprise changed to astonishment when he beheld the gunfighter reclining on both elbows and viewing the rampant warfare in a detached, almost bored, attitude.

Despite being outnumbered, the Russian soldiers were acquitting themselves superbly and wreaking havoc on the Union men. Drivers were able to start the motors on two of the jeeps, the two half-tracks, and two of the troop transports, and the vehicles started to execute turns so they could retreat out the gap.

Someone in the midst of the bedlam and the smoke, the flashes of gunfire and the yelling, was attempting to bellow orders.

Suddenly a new element was added to the battle. Blade heard more engines turn over, and he glanced over his right shoulder. The armored cars and pickups and the construction machinery were all rumbling from the parking lot. He looked to his right, where the two rows of Brount's men had stood minutes ago, and spotted only five or six still there. "Look out!" he shouted, but they couldn't hear him over the uproar.

The five cars and the three pickups closed on the Soviet convoy, the machine gunners in the cars and the men in the bed of each pickup pouring a torrent of lethal fire into the Russians. A pickup driver accidentally flattened one of Brount's men.

Dozens of soldiers were retreating on foot toward the gap, shooting in volleys as they went, slowing the pursuing Union forces down. The two half-tracks abruptly reversed direction. Instead of making for the gap, they turned and barreled toward the armored cars and the pickups.

Blade had to admire the Russian soldiers in the half-tracks. He knew they were buying time for their comrades to escape. Even as he watched, the nearest half-track gunner sent a withering burst into an onrushing armored car and the Union vehicle slewed to a stop and erupted in flames. An instant later the second half-track took out one of the pickups.

Ominous rumblings shook the very earth as the trio of construction machines lumbered forward, the bulldozer in the lead. They rolled inexorably toward the Soviets. Three troopers attempted to kill the bulldozer driver, standing their ground and firing their AK-47's, but their rounds smacked into the steel blade and richocheted. Obstinately they held firm, firing and firing, and they were still firing when the bulldozer ran over them, squishing them to a bloody pulp.

So far Blade hadn't fired a shot, and he had every intention of remaining where he was until the battle wound down. No one was paying the slightest attention to the Kid or him. He wasn't about to risk his life in a fight in which he didn't have a stake. That is, until he glimpsed a squad of six Russians making for the mansion.

Maddie was in there!

The Russian squad had slipped around the Force men, and they were now less than 15 yards from the front entrance.

Blade slapped the Kid's shoulder and leaned down to yell in the youth's left ear. "Come on!"

The Kid looked up, puzzled. "What?"

"Maddie!" Blade said, and pointed at the Russians.

Kid Zanto rose to a crouch, drawing the Redhawks as he

did, and nodded at the Warrior.

Stooping over at the waist, Blade raced toward the mansion, zigzagging as he ran, skirting bodies, ever alert for a threat. He scowled when he saw the Soviet squad enter the manor. "Damn!" he muttered to himself, and sprinted all out, heedless of his safety, bearing on a beeline for the front door. Ten feet from the entrance he distinctly heard the rattle of machine-gun fire from inside. He covered the remaining distance and threw himself to the right of the door.

The Kid darted to the left side.

Blade glanced back at the battlefield and beheld the bulldozer plowing into one of the half-tracks, and then he took a deep breath and rammed into the front door, which was ajar, sending it crashing inward.

Ahead in the corridor a Russian trooper stood over four bodies.

The Warrior squeezed the trigger, the Mandall bucking in his hands, and the trooper's chest was stitched by miniature geysers and he crumpled. Without missing a stride Blade plunged onward.

Gunshots and muffled shouts came from an upper floor.

Blade dashed up the stairwell, heading for the third floor, striding over three Union corpses as he ascended. He paused for a quick glimpse down the second hall and found only five Union bodies, and then he frantically sped higher, the Kid right on his heels. They were six steps below the third floor when to their ears came the terrified screech of a woman.

Maddie!

Blade cleared the final two steps and landed on the carpet, the Mandall leveled.

Six feet away, near an open door, were two Russians armed with AK-47's. They whirled toward him.

As fast as the troopers were, someone else was faster.

The Kid materialized on the Warrior's right and both Redhawks boomed even as Blade's fingers tightened on the

Mandall trigger.

Both soldiers were flung backwards into the corridor wall and sank to the floor, leaving bright red stains on the wall in their wake.

Blade and the Kid darted to the open door and, without a thought for their personal safety, rushed within to discover three dead Union men on the floor just inside and Maddie on her knees in the far corner, blood trickling from the right side of her mouth, while a Russian captain towered over her, about to slap her in the face. To the right were two soldiers coming through another doorway.

The Warrior and the gunfighter fired simultaneously, Blade shooting the captain in the back between the shoulder blades, the Kid slaying both soldiers with two snap shots to their heads.

Maddie scrambled to the left so the Russian captain wouldn't land on her as he slowly toppled forward, and then she was up and running to the Warrior and throwing her arms around him in gratitude. "Blade! Thank God!"

The Warrior held her at arm's length and stared at her split upper lip. "Are you okay?"

"A little sore," Maddie responded. "The Russian wanted to know where Crusher is. He thought I knew, and he intended to beat the information out of me."

"We've got to get you out of here," Blade said, and turned toward the corridor. "Kid?"

"Yeah?" the gunfighter responded, replacing the spent cartridges in his revolvers.

"I want you to take Maddie out of here."

"What?" Maddie responded before the Kid could answer.

"You heard me. This might be our only chance. In all the confusion the Kid can slip you out to the north. Once you're past the gravel mounds, find a spot to hide. I'll come for the two of you as soon as I can."

"I'm not leaving you," Maddie defied him.

"You can't stay," Blade insisted. "We've been all through

this. I have unfinished business to complete. I can't leave yet."

"Well, I'm not going either, then," Maddie said. "You're my friend, and I'm not about to—"

The window five feet away suddenly dissolved in a shattering shower of broken glass as wildly fired rounds from outside struck the glass.

"Duck!" Blade yelled, and instinctively dropped to his knees, raising his left forearm over his forehead to shield his eyes from the flying shards of glass. A heavy form fell onto his arm, and he looked up, horrified to discover Maddie sprawling on top of him. He dropped the Mandall and caught her under the arms, aghast at the sight of a hole above her right eye. "No!" he cried, and gently lowered her to the floor. "No!"

Outside the battle still raged. The continuous gunfire, the shouting, and the roaring of vehicle engines had attained a crescendo.

Blade knelt over Maddie Stender, dazed by her death. He reached out and closed her eyelids, sadness engulfing his soul. She must have glanced at the window at the moment the rounds hit, he realized, and been struck herself. He wanted to curl into a ball and not move for hours. Maddie had been a friend, one of the few he'd made in Shantytown. She'd stayed close to him to be of whatever help she could, and her selflessness had cost her her life. He looked at the Kid, kneeling nearby, and saw tears in the youth's eyes, and then he gazed at Maddie's placid features and his sorrow transformed into rage at the senselessness of her demise. Another decent, caring person had been butchered on the altar of violence. Would there never come an end to the bloodletting and the killing? Would there never be an era where all humankind lived in peace? Hadn't humanity learned *anything* from World War Three?

Kid Zanto abruptly rose and stalked into the corridor, the Redhawks held at waist level.

"Kid! Wait!" Blade called, and ran after the gunfighter when the youth wouldn't respond. He caught up with the Kid on the stairs. "Where are you going?"

"Out," the Kid said in a stern, gravelly tone.

"Why go anywhere? We're safer in here, and this isn't our fight. Let them kill each other off. It's no concern of ours."

"I feel like killin' some Commies."

Blade placed his right hand on the youth's shoulder, stopping him. "And what if you get killed?"

"So what?" Kid Zanto retorted, and jerked his shoulder free. He headed downward.

"Are you forgetting about Brount? If you're killed, who will repay him for your father?"

The Warrior's question caused the youth to halt in midstride.

"I'd like to run out and shoot Russians, too," Blade said, "but I have a mission to perform and the mission must come first. You can't permit your grief to make you reckless. Control the way you feel and channel all that emotional energy into achieving your revenge on Brount."

Zanto stared at the giant, his brow creased in contemplation. "All right," he stated after a minute. "I'll play this your way for now."

"Thanks," Blade responded, relieved the gunfighter wasn't about to foolishly throw his life away.

"So what's our next move?"

"Let's check and find out who's winning," Blade proposed, and together they descended to the bottom floor and moved toward the front door.

The Battle of the Gravel Pit, as the locals were later to refer to the conflict, had passed the critical point and was winding down. The Union had won. Corpses littered the battleground, as well as scores of wounded and the dying, whose pitiable moans and sobbing underscored the savagery of the confrontation. Sporadic gunshots boomed as the Union forces began moving up. To the east a group of 15 or 20 Russians had been herded into a compact circle with their arms in the air. Smoking, smoldering vehicles dotted the grounds. Three of the Union armored cars and one of the pickups had been destroyed. The Soviet convoy, with a notable exception, had become blazing wrecks. One of the half-tracks lay on its side. The other looked as if the bulldozer and the snowplow had rammed into it from both sides and crumpled the sturdy vehicle like a tin cup.

The Union forces manning the trenches on the gravel mounds had succeeded in stopping a troop transport at the mouth of the gap, blocking the exit and causing a logjam of Soviet vehicles. Unable to flee and hemmed in by the advancing Union men, the greatest number of Russian soldiers had died near the gap.

All three construction vehicles were at rest in the center of the grassy tract between the mansion and the pond. Heaps of Union dead were in evidence near the ditch. The two armored cars and the pair of pickups still functional were slowly threading a path among the bodies and the wrecks, the Union gunners finishing off injured Russians.

"I never figured war would be like this," the Kid said softly.

Blade stared at the only vehicle untouched by the battle, a Soviet troop transport, no less, that had not sustained so much as a scratch. He frowned at the irony. Or was it design? Because the only vehicle unaffected by the combat was the Russian truck containing the load of recently manufactured weapons.

"You know, this killin' business isn't all it's cracked up to be," Kid Zanto commented.

"I know," the Warrior agreed absently. He spied a cluster of men walking in the direction of the mansion, and he recognized Crusher Payne and Daniel Brount as being among them. With a start he realized he'd left the Mandall upstairs, so he unslug the Mossberg and gripped the shotgun tightly.

Time to get down to cases.

CHAPTER NINTEEN

The victorious Union leaders, consisting of Payne, Brount, and four other lieutenants, smiled and joked as they approached the mansion. Pelczar was with them, a confiscated AK-47 in his hands, and he was using the weapon to prod General Pronin in the back as he compelled the Russian commander to precede them.

"Hey, Blade! Kid!" Crusher called, and waved his right hand, beaming triumphantly. "Look who we caught!"

Blade nodded and glanced at the Kid. The youth had locked a baleful glare on Brount. "Not yet," he advised.

"Why not?" the Kid snapped impatiently.

"I need a few answers first," Blade informed him. "For me, Kid. Please."

The gunfighter frowned and sighed, then twirled the Redhawks into their holsters. "I wouldn't do this for anyone else," he groused.

"Thanks. I appreciate it," Blade said, then faced the Union leaders who were still ten feet off. "Where are the other lieutenants?" he asked.

Crusher Payne drew his right forefinger across his throat.

"I'll select new lieutenants later. Right now we're going to have some fun. Aren't we, pig?" he said, and kicked the Russian in the backside.

General Pronin hardly noticed the kick in the pants. He was staring at the Warrior in amazement, his eyes wide and his mouth slack.

"Aren't we, pig?" Crusher repeated, and lashed out with his right leg again, only this time his sole struck the Soviet officer behind the right knee and Pronin tripped and fell.

Brount and the lieutenants cackled.

"When I speak to you, you damn well better answer me!" Crusher barked at the Russian.

Blade had noticed the general's astounded gaze at seeing him, and he wondered if the Russian recognized him. The Warriors had fought the Soviets on several occasions, and Blade had penetrated deep into Russian-controlled territory twice on hazardous assignments, once all the way to Philadelphia and once to Cincinnati. The Russian commanders wanted the Warriors exterminated at all costs, and descriptions of Blade and a few fellow Warriors had been widely distributed.

"On your feet, pig!" Crusher directed.

General Pronin rose slowly, his countenance contorted in anger.

"Look at your convoy now, General," Crusher said, motioning at the corpses and the burning vehicles. "What happened to the vaunted Russian might? What happened to the invincible Russian army?" He paused. "You weren't so tough."

"You're a fool, Payne," General Pronin declared.

Crusher took a stride forward and backhanded the officer across the mouth. "*I'm* the fool? You're the one who waltzed right into my trap! You're the one who lost his whole command."

"You mentioned Russian might. Well, my command is as nothing compared to the full might of the Red Army, a fact you will no doubt discover in due course. Once I fail to return, an armored column will be sent to investigate. Our tanks and half-tracks will pound this gravel pit into dust."

"Big talk for the man on the losing end," Crusher said defiantly.

"Your juvenile posturings have assured the speedy downfall of the Union," General Pronin remarked. "Of course, you were destined to be eradicated anyway, sooner or later."

"What are you talking about?" Crusher inquired, his tone betraying a slight uncertainty.

General Pronin gazed over the battleground. "The Union is but one of many groups we have targeted for elimination."

"Why?"

"Because we intend to expand our domination," General Pronin answered. "Our leaders want to push north to the Great Lakes in Wisconsin and Michigan. The strategic advantages stemming from the shipping lanes alone are tremendous."

"You plan to wipe out the Union?" Crusher queried, stunned by the news.

"And anyone else who stands in our path of conquest," the Russian declared. "We have stood still for far too long, and we intend to remedy our stagnation by stepping up our timetable."

"You'll never defeat the Union," Crusher boasted.

"Don't flatter yourselves," General Pronin said. "The Union is no more than a pimple on the ass of humanity, a pimple we will pop when the time comes."

Crusher glanced over his right shoulder at the mopping up operation, and the sight of the defeated Russians restored his confidence. He looked at the general and smirked. "We'll be ready for anything you throw at us."

"Will you?" Pronin countered, and snorted. "You'll be too busy dealing with those who will arise to challenge your control of this region."

"What do you mean?"

"Have you ever heard of the Doctrine of Destabilization?"

Crusher shook his head.

"Of course you haven't," General Pronin said, with the condescending air of an adult explaining an important issue to a mere child. "Then allow me to elaborate. The Doctrine of Destablization is a time-honored and proven method of destroying an enemy nation or state from within. Success is inevitable. All one has to do is follow the three steps." He held up a finger. "One, you identify subversive elements within the country or state you want to conquer. You stir them up and fan their hate." He extended a second finger. "Two, you supply every element with all the arms they need." A third finger rose. "And three, you sit back and wait for them to finish killing one another off. Even if the rebel elements do not overthrow the existing government or authority, they will so weaken the existing political and civil heirarchy that conquest will be easily accomplished." Pronin lowered his hand and grinned. "Elementary, yes?"

Blade could see the intense concentration reflected on Crusher Payne's features.

"So that's why you agreed to supply us with arms," Crusher said slowly, "and Harland Warner too."

"And others unknown to you," General Pronin disclosed.

Crusher looked at the Russian. "Why are you telling me all this?"

"For two reasons. First, your knowledge of our plan will not effect the outcome. We will extend our boundaries all the way to the Great Lakes, and there is nothing you can do to stop us."

"What's the second reason?"

General Pronin smiled. "To convince you of my sincerity so you will accept my offer."

"Offer?" Crusher repeated quizzically.

"Yes. I offer you critical information in exchange for my life and the lives of my men who have survived," General Pronin said.

"What critical information?" Crusher asked testily. "Why the hell should I spare any of you bastards?"

The Russian shrugged. "I thought perhaps you would be interested in learning the identity of a spy among you."

"A spy?" Crusher grabbed the front of the officer's uniform and pulled Pronin off balance. "There has been a Commie spy among us all the time?" he demanded, livid at the very idea.

"Not one of ours," General Pronin said, trying to pry Payne's fingers from his shirt.

Crusher shoved the Russian from him. "Then who is this spy? Where does he come from?"

"Have we a deal?" General Pronin inquired, smoothing his uniform.

"Depends on your information."

"That is not good enough," the officer stated. "I want your word my life will be spared, and the lives of my men, or you can kill me now and be done with it."

Blade saw Crusher's eyes narrow, and he knew the Union leader was gauging the Russian's resolve. The Warrior scanned the five-acre area, noting the numbers and positions of the Union forces.

Crusher exchanged glances with Dan Brount, who nodded, and stared at General Pronin. "All right. You've got yourself a deal. I'll spare your life and the lives of any of your men still alive. But if you're jerking me around . . ."

The Russian held up his right hand. "I give you my word the information I am about to reveal is true."

"It'd better be," Crusher muttered.

General Pronin cleared his throat. "Have you ever heard of the Freedom Federation?"

"Rings a vague bell," Crusher said.

"I think I have," Brount interjected.

The Russian deliberately refrained from looking in the Warrior's direction. He sidled closer to the Union leaders. "The Freedom Federation is a confederation of seven members who seem to believe they have the right to run this land in the manner they see fit."

Blade listened while surveying the jumble of vehicles near

the gap.

"I will be honest with you and tell you they are our enemies," General Pronin told Crusher. "But they are also your enemies. They want to reestablish order and peace in this country, and they are opposed to any group that tries to lord it over others."

The Warrior counted 59 Union men, a third of whom were injured. Fifteen were guarding the captured soldiers. Another 15 or 20 were tending to the wounded. Leaving ten or so who were walking around the open area, checking on the bodies and gathering weapons into piles.

"The two largest members of the Freedom Federation are the Free State of California and the Civilized Zone," General Pronin was saying. "Another faction, the Flathead Indian Tribe, is based in the former state of Montana. The Dakota territory is under the control of a group of horsemen called the Cavalry. And the three remaining members are all located in northern Minnesota."

"What does all this have to do with us?" Crusher Payne asked.

"Be patient and I will get to that," the officer said, annoyed. "Now, where was I? Oh, yes. In the former town of Halma, in northern Minnesota, live refugees from the Twin Cities who call themselves the Clan. Only seventy or eighty miles away live the Moles, descendants of a survivalist group, who live in an underground city of tunnels and caverns. And last, but by no means least, is the Federation faction known as the Family. They live in a fortified compound situated somewhere between the Clan and the Moles."

"I still don't see the point," Crusher snapped.

"Certain members of the Family are designated as Warriors, and these Warriors are entrusted with the defense of their compound and the protection of the Family. They also will oppose any threats to the welfare of the Freedom Federation," Pronin detailed.

"So?" Crusher said.

Blade glanced at the Kid and intentionally spoke before the officer could answer. "Hey, Kid."

Everyone focused on the giant.

"What the hell are you doing?" Crusher demanded. "Don't interrupt us."

"Sure thing," Blade said, and smiled. Then, to their utter consternation, he ignored Payne. "Hey, Kid."

"Yeah?" the youthful gunfighter replied, perplexed by his friend's behavior.

"What the hell is this?" Crusher growled.

"I have the answers I needed, " Blade said.

"You do?" the Kid responded.

"Blade!" Crusher barked angrily.

"Yes, I do," the Warrior confirmed. "So whenever you want to finish it, be my guest."

"Finish what?" Brount spoke up, mystified.

"Thanks," the Kid said.

"Anytime," Blade replied.

"Will someone tell me what's going on here?" Crusher Payne requested gruffly.

"I can," Blade cheerfully offered.

"*You* can?" Crusher queried in confusion.

"Yep, I can," Blade said, his left hand on the slide action, his right on the pistol grip.

"This I've got to hear," Crusher declared.

"I would like to leave now," General Pronin chimed in eagerly.

"You're not going anywhere, you lousy double-crosser," Crusher responded.

"Then I am a dead man," the Russian lamented, his eyes on the AK-47 trained on his abdomen by Pelczar.

"I don't understand any of this," a lieutenant commented.

"You will," Blade promised.

Crusher Payne held his arms aloft. "Everyone *shut up*!"

No one spoke.

"That's more like it," Crusher said, and gazed at the Warrior. "Now you were going to tell us something?"

"Certainly," Blade said, and nodded at General Pronin. "The Russians sold the guns to you."

"Guns?" Crusher repeated.

Blade nodded at Payne. "And you distributed the guns among your lieutenants."

"What guns?" Crusher asked.

The Warrior nodded at Daniel Brount. "You sold some of the weapons to members of a gang of raiders who were passing through Shantytown."

"What the hell is he talking about?" Crusher roared, glaring at his lieutenants, then the giant.

"The raiders made their way into northern Minnesota," Blade related, his voice lowering sadly, "where they ambushed four Mole families who were on an outing."

"Moles! *Moles*!" Crusher shouted. "What the hell do the damned Moles have to do with this?"

"Everything," Blade answered. "The Moles tracked down the raiders and extracted information before killing them, information about the new guns the raiders had used. The Mole leader sent for me and after he filled me in I decided to head directly to Shantytown by myself and work undercover to trace the weapons to their source."

"Why would the leader of the Moles . . . ?" Crusher began, then caught himself, dumbfounded as a degree of comprehension dawned.

Blade straightened to his full height, his visage a grim mask. "Wolfe sent for me because I'm the man the Freedom Federation relies on to dispose of threats and problems. I'm also the head of the Warriors." He paused, and then mimicked the tone Crusher Payne had used when greeting Maddie. "But you can call me Blade, you suck-egg, lowlife, egotistical, pissant son of a bitch."

CHAPTER TWENTY

For the space of three seconds no one moved. The Union men were rooted in place, stupefied by the giant's revelation. Palczar still seemed confused, and he looked at Crusher Payne.

General Pronin, seeing the bodyguard momentarily distracted, took the opportunity to whirl and flee, precipitating the bloodbath.

Acting on pure reflex, glimpsing the Russian officer out of the corner of his eye, Pelczar squeezed the trigger, sending a dozen rounds boring into General Pronin's back, the impact flinging the commander to the grass in a disjointed tangle of arms and legs.

Even as Pelczar fired, Blade shoved the Mossberg barrel into Crusher Payne's face and let the Union leader have a full load of buckshot at point-blank range. The effect was the same as that of a ten-pound rock striking a soggy pumpkin. Blood, brains, and hair sprayed everywhere, causing the four lieutenants to automatically shield their eyes from the spattering gore. Blade shot each of them in the chest.

Only Daniel Blount had disregarded the fleshy chunks

striking him. He saw the Warrior pivot to shoot his four companions, and he whipped the double-action 45's from their holsters, grinning in anticipation, knowing there was no way Blade could get him before he planted four shots in the Warrior's gut. At the moment he drew he saw Kid Zanto, standing off to the left, going for those Ruger Redhawks. From then on everything appeared to unfold in slow motion. Somehow the Kid cleared leather first, but instead of aiming the big revolvers at the giant, the Kid swung them at Brount!

One of the other lieutenants was screaming.

Flabbergasted, Brount saw the Kid's mouth move and thought he heard the words, "For my dad!" And then those Redhawks thundered, and Brount felt a searing pain in his chest and an invisible hand shoved him backwards, stumbling but erect, until the big revolvers boomed yet again. A sledgehammer slammed into Brount's forehead and he catapulted to the turf, his consciousness sinking into a Stygian abyss.

Pelczar, gawking at the fallen Crusher Payne, had not moved to defend himself.

The Warrior took a quick stride and rammed the shotgun barrel against the bodyguard's left temple, and Pelczar dropped on the spot.

"What now?" the Kid asked, staring at Brount's corpse.

Blade scrutinized the gravel pit. The Russian prisoners, the Union men guarding them, the injured and those ministering to them, the hired guns mopping up, and the three construction machinery drivers, who were standing near the steam shovel, all were frozen, transfixed by the tableau of their leaders dying. The two armored cars and the two pickups were idling near the pond. "This is my fight," he said.

"You wish," the Kid replied, grinning impishly.

"Don't say I didn't warn you," Blade said, grinning back, and then he ran forward, heading toward the construction equipment, toward the Monster Machines.

The Kid raced even with the Warrior.

Without any leadership the Union men were confounded by the turn of events. They looked at one another, as if each was waiting for someone else to rally them, to make the first move.

The captured Soviet soldiers seized the moment and pounced on the Union guards, and a general melee erupted.

A few Union killers began firing at the Warrior and the gunfighter.

Blade heard a round smack into the ground to his right, and he doubled over and darted to the left, then to the right, hoping to throw the marksman off.

"What's your plan?" the Kid queried, staying on the giant's heels.

"Can you take out anyone who tries to stop me?"

"You've got it," the Kid vowed, and promptly suited action to words by halting and firing his left Ruger twice.

Twenty yards to the left a man screeched, clutched at his head, and toppled over.

Blade focused on his destination: the construction equipment. He saw the drivers scrambling to climb into their machines, and he poured on the speed, making for the gigantic snowplow. Of the three, he reasoned he would experience the least difficulty driving the snowplow. He'd driven automatic and manual-transmission vehicles before, and he calculated the stick shift in the snowplow might be similar to the stick shifts in Federation trucks he had handled.

The raucous rumble of revving motors rent the air as the two armored cars and the pickups peeled out from near the pond and bore down on the racing duo.

Move! his mind shrieked, and Blade sprinted all out, his boots pounding on the turf, his legs flying. Fifteen yards separated him from his destination when he heard the snowplow kick over, and the next instant the behemoth lumbered straight at him. He threw himself to the right, and as he landed he saw the two armored cars and the two pickups appear off to the right, zooming his way.

The bulldozer operator was striving to start his machine,

while the steam shovel operator had just reached the cabin of his.

Kid Zanto had halted ten yards back and faced the onrushing cars and trucks, a grin curling his thin lips, the Rugers extended.

With its motor roaring, the snowplow came directly at the Warrior.

Blade had a single shell remaining in the Mossberg. From where he lay in the grass, he could see the steam shovel operator working the controls. He would have preferred to be closer, but he angled the shotgun upwards, sighted, and fired.

The windshield in the steam shovel burst into a thousand fragments, and the shovel operator staggered backwards, his arms flailing, and fell from view.

There was no time to lose! The snowplow was less than eight yards off! Blade slung the Mossberg over his right shoulder, rising into a crouch, and peered up at the massive yellow plow almost on top of him. The top of the plow screened him from the driver's line of sight. He scuttled away from the blade, skirting the plow, keeping low so the driver couldn't spot him. Once past the plow he cut sharply to the left, and in four bounds reached the driver's door. He grabbed the handle and yanked, and the door flew wide open.

The shocked driver looked at the giant jogging alongside his cab, and then tried to pull the door shut.

Blade wasn't about to let him. He grasped the driver's wrist and heaved, and the man shot from the cab like a missile and crunched headfirst onto the ground. The Warrior caught at the door frame and hauled himself into the vehicle. He gripped the steering wheel as the enormous piece of equipment lurched and bucked. To his right was a stick shift, and on the floor a pair of pedals, the exact same setup as the troop trucks he'd driven! He tramped on the proper pedal and ground the gears into second, and only then did he look up, through the windshield, and his blood changed to ice.

Kid Zanto stood directly in the path of the snowplow, less

than eight feet from the tip of the plow, firing at the armored cars and the pickups, oblivious to the danger. The closest vehicle was one of the pickups, zeroing in on the gunfighter from the left, approximately 40 feet distant.

Working his arms in a frenzy, Blade wrenched on the steering wheel and sent the snowplow into a tight turn to the left. He saw the plow narrowly miss the Kid, who glanced up in alarm and dove to the right. Blade clasped the steering wheel firmly, locking the motorized goliath on course, and seconds later his maneuver succeeded: The plow rammed into the closest pickup, shearing into the metal with the ease of a knife through butter. The pickup buckled and broke into sections, the occcupants screeching as they died.

One down, four to go.

Blade straightened the steering wheel and floored the gas pedal, grinning as the massive wheels churned toward an armored car 50 feet away. The car had stopped, and the machine gunner was squeezing down through the square opening into the back seat. Blade had no idea what they were up to. Perhaps they hadn't witnessed the snowplow demolish the pickup. Perhaps they were planning to head for the hills. He was not in a mood to care. The speedometer indicated 45 miles an hour when the point of the plow smashed through the passenger door and impaled the armored car.

The men never had a prayer.

Blade slammed the stick shift into reverse, and the engine hardly strained as the snowplow backed up and disengaged itself from the wreckage with much grinding and rasping.

Two down.

He angled toward the center of the open area, scanning for the other vehicles. To the east Russian soldiers and Union men were still fighting, hand to hand. Other Union men were assisting injured fellows in trying to reach the gap and presumed safety. Sixty feet ahead an armored car raced in hot pursuit of a pair of fleeing Russians who were making for the north.

Neither soldier made it.

The machine gunner in the car opened fire, and he was skilled at his job. The slugs ripped into the pair of Russians and toppled them in a pile. The driver braked so the gunner could insure their victims were dead.

Bad move.

The snowplow hit the armored car from the rear and drove the trunk all the way into the engine compartment, squishing the two men into a pasty glob of reddish goo. Again Blade threw the machine into reverse, and as he straightened the wheel, bullets smacked into the windshield. He shifted into first, searching for the source, and spotted the last pickup 70 feet off. Two men in the bed were peppering the snowplow with automatic fire. He turned toward them, but the lighter, faster pickup cut back on itself and came at him from another direction.

Smart move.

Blade shifted and tried to bear down on the pickup, and again the smaller vehicle handily evaded him. How could he catch them when—

A tremendous crash shook the snowplow and the entire machine tilted at a crazy slant as the passenger-side tires were lifted into the air.

Startled, Blade glanced to his right, leaning toward the passenger door for a better look. What he saw made the hairs on the nape of his neck stand on end.

The bulldozer had rammed him!

The Warrior saw the bulldozer operator look at him and grin wickedly, then apply himself to the controls in an effort to have the bulldozer shove the snowplow completely over. Blade knew he couldn't obtain traction with half of his tires suspended. He was a sitting duck for any Union killer who came along. A round punched a neat hole in the windshield, reminding him the pickup was still after him, and he gazed to his right to discover the pickup hurtling at him at a great rate of speed. They must figure he was pinned and helpless, and they'd be on him in ten seconds unless he did something, *anything*, to force the bulldozer operator to release the snowplow. He's used all the shells in the Mossberg. . . .

But the guy operating the bulldozer didn't know that!

Blade unslung the shotgun with his right hand and leaned toward the passenger side again. He extended his arm and pointed the Mossberg at the bulldozer operator.

The man did a double take and blanched. He desperately manipulated the controls, sending the bulldozer rearward.

Blade smiled when the snowplow bounced onto all its tires, and he tramped on the accelerator, getting out of there before the bulldozer could come at him again. To his right the pickup roared in pursuit, the men in the bed firing indiscriminately. He let go of the steering wheel, allowing the juggernaut to proceed undirected, and hurriedly reloaded the shotgun.

If they wanted a piece of him so much, he'd give them a piece!

He shifted the loaded shotgun to his left hand and resumed steering with his right.

The pickup came up fast on the driver's side, the machine gunners going for the cab.

Blade ducked as low as he could, counted to three, then straightened and found the pickup nearly broadside with his door. He simply pointed the barrel at the pickup cab and squeezed the trigger.

Careening uncontrollably, the pickup slewed to the left, then the right, and the men in the bed screamed when they spied the smoldering wreck of a half-track directly in their path. They tried to bail out, but they were just clearing the bed when the pickup smashed into the half-track and both went up in a brilliant, fiery blast.

Four down.

Leaving only the bulldozer.

Where was it?

Blade slowed, glancing to the right and the left, front and back, and he saw the bulldozer 40 yards to his rear and closing. So the operator still wanted to play! He executed a tight turn and arrowed the tip of the plow at the bulldozer.

The operator perceived the Warrior's tactic and did what

any man who wanted to live would do. He jumped.

Blade wasn't interested in the driver. He wanted the bulldozer out of commission, and he intended to ram the machine until he happened to look toward the mansion and abruptly changed his mind. No, he couldn't destroy the snowplow yet, not when work was unfinished. Instead, he held on tightly to the wheel and slanted the snowplow at the bulldozer, aligning the plow with the rear of the other Monster Machine. He braced for the impact, and the entire truck shook when the plow hit, the edge of the snowplow shearing into the back of the bulldozer and ripping off the treads, portions of the undercarriage, and a car-sized segment of the motor housing.

Black smoke billowed from the crippled bulldozer, and the machine ground to a halt, sputtering and sparking.

The Warrior turned the snowplow toward the mansion, and his features hardened into steely lines. If he left anything standing, any vestige of the Union's power and prestige, they would regroup and reassert their tyranny over the region. Maybe, just maybe, they wouldn't be so quick to reorganize if the symbol of their former supremacy were utterly destroyed. He steered for the front entrance.

A lone, stocky figure rose in his path, 30 yards in front of him, an AK-47 in the figure's hands.

Pelczar!

Blade grinned and adjusted his direction so the snowplow would conveniently crush the bodyguard. Surprise altered his expression when Pelczar lifted the AK-47 overhead and disdainfully flung the weapon aside. His gray eyes narrowed a second later as Pelczar shook a huge right fist at the snowplow, and calmly and slowly moved to the left out of the behemoth's line of travel.

A challenge?

He concentrated on the distance separating the mansion from the snowplow, appreciating that timing would be critical. His eyes flitted once toward the shattered window on the third floor, and he frowned as he opened the door and shoved, then tensed his legs and leaped, the Mossberg in his left hand. He hit the ground hard on his shoulders and tumbled end over end, unable to arrest his momentum, his sense of direction askew, and finally came to rest in a sitting posture, dazed, facing the manor.

The snowplow was almost there.

A thrill ran up and down the Warrior's spine as he watched the mammoth Monster Machine plow into the front entrance, a stupendous projectile of unstoppable force tearing through the very bowels of the Union headquarters, ripping apart wood and stone and brick and mortar, knocking down wall after wall, breaking down support beams, and causing the central section of the structure to collapse upon itself. The noise was stupendous. He smiled wearily, pleased at his handiwork, and went to rise.

Powerful hands clamped on his neck from the rear and he was hauled brutally to his feet. "Bastard!" bellowed a gravelly voice. "Die, you bastard!"

Blade let go of the Mossberg and reached behind him, grasping a pair of sturdy wrists. He dropped to his left knee, at the same time snapping his shoulders down and whipping those wrists forward. Someone arced over his head and sprawled onto the grass, but swiftly recovered. The Warrior stood and regarded his foe. "Pelczar."

"I plan to kill you with my bare hands!" the bodyguard snarled.

"Your master is dead. Why go through with this?"

Pelczar crouched, his fists clenching and unclenching. "I'm a Union man. I've always been a Union man. Thanks to Mister Payne, I became important and respected. I owe the Union for everything I am, and I always pay my dues."

"Is that your only reason?"

"I hate your guts."

"I have no desire to kill you. You're a pawn, a dupe. . . ." Blade began.

Pelczar uttered an inarticulate growl and charged, swinging his pile-driver fists savagely.

Blade backpedaled, blocking the initial blows, wishing he could end the fight quickly. He took a glancing blow to the left cheek and planted a right fist in Pelczar's stomach.

The bodyguard barely slowed.

Countering punch after punch, jab after jab, Blade continued to retreat, making the bodyguard bring the fight to him, making Pelczar expend the most energy.

"I'll kill you!" Pelczar unexpectedly bellowed.

Blade had encountered few men who would be the bodyguard's equal in raw strength. His forearms ached from just blocking the rain of punches, and he could feel the strain in his shoulders and neck. Still he fought on, giving as good as he got. Once his right landed on the tip of Pelczar's chin and rocked the man on his heels.

The bodyguard halted the assault and stepped back, breathing heavily. "You're the best I've ever met."

"You're not shabby yourself," Blade responded, then put a smirk on his face, "for an amateur."

Pelczar roared and attacked anew.

For minutes they slugged and smashed, punched and pounded, and neither seemed destined to best the other until a mishap occurred.

Blade was taking a shuffling pace backwards when his left heel connected with a Union corpse and he went down, landing on his back. As he fell, he saw Pelczar whip aside the flaps of the brown jacket and go for a pair of Desert Eagle .357's. He instantly threw himself to the right, drawing the Bowies as he rolled, and he came up on his knees with his arms back and tensed for the toss. Too late.

The bodyguard stood four feet away, his arms extended, the .357's cocked, grinning maliciously. "Suckered you, sucker!" he gloated.

Blade knew Pelczar would squeeze those triggers in another instant, and his body went rigid in expectation of being shot. But in the millisecond before the guns would have boomed, a youthful voice shouted from somewhere off to the right.

"Pelczar!"

Distracted for the briefest instant, the bodyguard flicked his eyes in the direction of the shout, then back again, but he had already given the Warrior a fleeting moment to react.

And react Blade did, bringing both arms down in a double throw, and even as the hilts left his hands he was already in motion, diving to the right again. He heard the Desert Eagles blast three times, and he shoved to his feet and prepared to spring in a headlong rush. Only the fight was over.

Pelczar stood with his legs wide, his arms still extended, the barrels of the .357's drooping, his confounded gaze on the twin hilts protruding from the center of his broad chest. He looked at the Warrior and tried to speak, but blood bubbled from his mouth and he staggered forward two strides. The Desert Eagles fell from limp fingers.

Blade walked up to the bodyguard and placed his hands on the Bowie hilts. "I believe these are mine," he said, and wrenched the knives out.

Pelczar the bodyguard pitched onto his face.

CHAPTER TWENTY-ONE

They stood over the freshly dug grave, their hands clasped in front of them, their sorrowful eyes on the mound of brown dirt.

"I ain't much good at this sort of thing," the Kid said.

"Then I'll do the honors," Blade offered, and lifted his gaze to the morning sky. "We commend the soul of our sister, Maddie Stender, to your care, Oh, Spirit. She was a loyal friend who knew how to give of herself to those in need. We pray that you will guide her in the higher mansions as you did in this world. Amen."

Kid Zanto glanced at the Warrior in surprise. "Where'd you learn those fancy words?"

"From the Family Elders."

"I'd like to meet them sometime," the Kid remarked.

Blade looked at the two saddled horses waiting ten feet to the left. Except for the animals and themselves, nothing stirred in the gravel pit. They were the last to leave. All the Russians and Union men had fled, taking their wounded with them. "You can," he said. "Come with me to the Home."

The Kid chewed on his lower lip, then sighed. "I thought

about comin'. I like the idea of livin' someplace where I don't have to worry about a scavenger or a mutant leapin' from behind every bush. But I can't."

"Susie?"

"Yep. I'm going back to Shantytown and takin' her out of that dive."

"And then?"

"And then I figure on headin' to my dad's farm and takin' up where he left off," the Kid said.

Blade smiled and stretched out his right arm. "I hope the two of you find true happiness together. If you change your mind, bring Susie to the Home. I'm positive I can persuade the Elders to allow you to live at our compound. We can always use a man like you in the Warriors."

"I'll keep it in mind," the Kid pledged, and walked to his horse. He mounted slowly, surveyed the corpses and the wreckage, then wheeled his mount and headed for the gap.

The Warrior climbed on the black stallion, stared sadly at the grave a final time, and rode to the east. He passed between the towering gravel mounds, not bothering to pause and look behind him, riding from the valley of the shadow into the dawn of a new day, heading for the Home and those he loved.